CALHOUN

PERRY'S NEST BOOK 3

KATHI S. BARTON

World Castle Publishing, LLC
Pensacola, Florida
Copyright © Kathi S. Barton 2023
Hardback ISBN: 9798393908553
Paperback ISBN: 9781960076687
eBook ISBN: 9781960076694
First Edition World Castle Publishing, LLC, May 8, 2023
http://www.worldcastlepublishing.com

Prologue

"Since they're considered non-lethal weapons in most of the United States and Puerto Rico, you can carry them around with you pretty much anyplace you go. And now that you've taken the classes on them, you can feel good about using it too." Rosie picked up her new purchase and liked the weight of it in her hand. She'd not gone for the girly pink or camo but the plain flat black taser she had been using. "Since the hospital has offered the classes here and you've purchased one, you get a discount to buy other items you might want to consider carrying around. I heard this is your last day."

"It is. I'm traveling to Ohio over the next month

and then working up there at a larger hospital. I worked there a few years ago." She put the taser in her backpack and made her way to the elevator while saying goodbye to the officer who had been helping her. "See you around."

More than likely, she'd not. Rosie had been at this hospital as a traveling nurse for the last seven months. There wasn't anything at all she liked here but the very little view she got of the ocean from her camper in the early morning.

She was done with this area. Not only that, but she thought that this particular hospital would be out of business soon the way they did things around here, like the lack of security for their staff. Not to mention, it was in the worst kind of neighborhood for any place she'd ever been.

Three nights ago, a group of nurses leaving work had been attacked. Even before that, there had been a man who came into the place through one of the exit doors from the kitchen and stole a lot of meat. The hospital's solution to it never happening again was to tell them they needed to be more careful. Fuck that shit, she thought. I'm out of here at the end of the night.

Getting on the elevator, she was glad that the place had good air conditioning around it. The floor she'd been working on, Labor and Delivery, had had theirs going off and on for the last few hours. It would be a hot one for women delivering today if she didn't miss her bet. The man that entered the elevator just as the doors were closing had her backing away.

"Where are the babies?" She asked him what he'd said. "The babies. Where do they keep them after they're born? That woman down there wouldn't give me no answers unless I told her a name. I just want to go and see the babies. They calm me."

Alarms went off in her mind. Telling him that L&D was on the fourth floor instead of the second, she pushed the button for four. He asked her where the mommas were then. She said they'd be on the fifth. Not sure what to do now, Rosie pulled her backpack closer around her body and used it as a shield around her front. She only hoped that her lies to the man would give her enough time to be able to warn people of what might be coming their way.

While he was looking at the elevator numbers get larger, she pulled out her taser and held it in her hand the way she'd been taught. Not having any clue what was going on right now, she just knew that she'd feel better if she was able to protect herself and those babies that were on the second floor if necessary. As soon as the door opened to the fourth floor, the man reached up behind him, pulled out a sawed-off shotgun and brought it forward.

~*~

Rosie pulled out her service revolver and cell phone and laid them on the little table beside her. She'd tried to take a little nap when she'd gotten home earlier but was too upset to last more than a few minutes at the futile attempt. Joey was laying at her feet right now, soaking up the sunshine and drying his thick fur.

"I think that bear shifter sees more than anyone else. He sure got my number in a hurry." Joey just whined at her. He wasn't much of a talker. "Last time I was able to be that free with my words, it was my sister. What do you suppose she's doing right now?"

Nothing from the peanut gallery. Looking up when she heard something backfire, Rosie put her gun back on the table without even realizing that she'd picked it up again. When it was safe where it was, she went back to thinking about Ruby.

Ruby was her younger sister by four years. Not that she ever acted like she was the younger of the two of them. People had thought they'd been born twins and that they were tight as sisters could be. They were tight, that was for sure, but only because Ruby had a way of calling her up and bashing her for whatever had been in her head. Almost like they were having an out-of-body experience talking to each other, and Ruby would call to get the final word in. She even started the conversations off like that.

No hello, or how are you. But right to the part where Rosie was either having a shitty day or she was thinking thoughts that Ruby thought Rosie had no right to, like ending her life. It had been a real struggle all her life to keep going. It hadn't gotten any better when she'd gotten out of college nor even when she'd enlisted in the service. But last night had been the worst.

Glancing at her phone when it chirped, she let it go to voice mail. It was the cop again. The one that had talked to her when she'd been having her breakfast. Joey stood up and came to her, putting his head on her leg while she petted him.

"I'm all right, boy. That wasn't her." When he seemed satisfied that she was indeed all right, he laid back down at her feet. "I wonder what she'd do if she were here now, Joey? Would she be cursing up a storm or in the camper making me something nastily good for me to eat? I think both. How about you?"

She looked out over the sea of campers and wondered at the ungodly amount of money sitting in ankle-deep sand and spiders. Not to mention the chairs, flip-flops and towels. The kids, too, were forever leaving their shit either on the walk to the beach or on the beach that ended up around some unsuspecting animal. Shaking her head, Rosie decided that she was going to have better thoughts for the next five minutes.

"Have you seen my doggie?" Rosie shook her head at the woman who lived in the camper not far from where she was. "He's come up missing. Poor old thing. He don't hear well, and I'm afraid one of them sharks came up and got him. Poor old thing."

Rosie didn't know what the elderly woman's story was and usually didn't offer up any kind of ideas about where the dog had gone. If she had been honest with herself, she hadn't ever seen the thing and couldn't have been able to tell anyone if she knew what color it was. Going back to her thinking good thoughts, a group of kids came around the corner of the lane she was in, scattering up sand and shells all over the place. Rosie chose to ignore them. But the man on the other side didn't.

He did this about four times a week when a new group of campers would come into the lot and disturb his vacation. He'd pull out the hose, turn the water on and spray the shit out of the kids. Twice now, the police had been called on him because the water in the hose would get scalding hot and burn the kids. She looked for a lawsuit soon enough, and Rosie was going to sit back and watch it all come about. If she was still here, she told herself. Then she thought about her sister.

They'd grown up in an all-right home. Both their parents had worked full-time. Came home to cook dinner together, then they'd watch a little television and go to bed. If homework wasn't finished up by the time dinner was, dad or mom, or sometimes both of them, would help with that while the kitchen waited until later.

Her phone sounded again, and she resisted the urge to turn it off. It was the cop again, not her sister. If she turned it off and Ruby couldn't get in touch with her, she'd send the police to find her and then make her call her back. It was a game, one that Rosie was getting tired of playing of late.

Their holidays were wonderful. Big dinners for each of them. A large tree at Christmas time. Vacations to places that most families only read about. Even when they traveled around as she was now, their parents had made a wonderful time of it. They'd have weekend trips too. To places like zoos and amusement parks. Every child's wish and then some.

Then her father had gotten killed. Just a random shooting at a convenience store that not only cost his life but that of four others in the building. Mom took it hard, and they had to move in with her parents. Life took an abrupt change on that night, and she and her sister never had a good child life after that.

"Of course, I was seventeen by then and should have figured out my life before that. I mean, it was too good for too long, don't you think?" Joey huffed at her, something that he did on occasion. "You know the stories. I couldn't get my head out of my ass to save my life, and it cost me. And my mother."

Mom had committed suicide just after Ruby had turned eighteen. The note she left them said that she didn't want to be around any longer and wanted to be with their dad. He had been and would always be her world. That hit them both hard, having thought that they were their world when they were growing up. Rosie's life took a tumble, and it had been almost too late for her to get back on the right path toward the end of it.

This time when her phone rang, Ruby's face appeared. Picking up the phone, she was sobbing before she could even say hello. It took her a few minutes to realize what her sister was saying to her when she was able to calm down.

"I said where are you? I'm here in this god-awful park you're in, and I don't know where to find you." She told her the lot number she was in. "Good, not too far from me. What are you doing not at work? I thought you had another week to go."

Just as she was about to tell her what had happened and the date today, she saw her sister pull into the place next to her camper. Rushing to her, nearly tripping over Joey to get to her, the two of them hugged and talked all over each other until they had to sit down. Joey was excited to see Ruby as she was, and they bonded while she sat there looking at the two of them.

"I had a feeling that you were in trouble. Then early this morning, I had a feeling that you needed me. I don't know what prompted me to come to this place, other than it's cheap and run down, but I found you. I'm going to stay with you for a while if that's all right with you two." She asked her sister what was wrong. "Always right to the point, aren't you? I'm dying. I have a brain tumor about the size of a golf ball that can't be operated on."

She was stunned to silence. Her thoughts on ending her life circled around in her head as she sat there. And now her sister was going to die through no fault of her own. Not sure what she could say to her baby sister, she sat there while she talked to Joey and told him what a good dog he was being.

"When did you find out?" She told her a few days ago. She'd been having a lot of blackouts and went to see the doctor. "I hope you saw a specialist. Someone other than just a doctor. I'm not saying that they're not right. But a second opinion wouldn't hurt."

"I've seen several specialists. Not to mention surgeons, as well as anything else that I had hoped to get better news from. All of them say the same thing. The tumor has advanced to the point where it's too large and set in to be taken out without leaving me with nothing more than just a dead brain." She nearly said that she would take that but didn't. But losing her sister was more than she could think of right now.

"I know someone." She asked her if he was a miracle worker. "He might be. He's the responding officer to the trouble at the hospital. Not that he was a cop but a psychiatrist that was…never mind. That's not what is important. He's a shifter. You can be healed if you allow him to change you." Her sister was already shaking her head. "No, don't do that. I can't lose you, Ruby. You're all I have in the world, and you keep me balanced."

Picking up her phone, she made the call to the doctor who had left her several messages. Not bothering with looking at them, she redialed his number and talked to Ruby. Things had to be better for her sister. If for no other reason than that she —

"You're a very difficult woman to get in touch with." She told him where she was and that he had to come to her right now. "Are you all right? Did something happen?"

"No. I mean, yes. Just come here. My sister is here, and I'd like for you to meet her. I need something from you to save her life." The silence was very telling, and she started to cry. "You can turn me down when you get here. But right now, I need for you to come and talk with her so that you can see if you can help her. She's all I have in the world right now, and I can't lose her. You have to come."

As they waited for him to come to them, Rosie

ordered pizza. It was a good place to get food from, and they delivered. While she was taking care of that, Ruby went into her camper and started fussing at her about how messy it was.

It really was. But she'd been working so much to get this job under her belt that she didn't care. Now she could see that she'd left things to go. Even having a washer and dryer in the place, she'd not done any laundry other than what had to be done. Helping her clean up things, she was glad now that she was going to have clean sheets on her bed for the two of them. Tonight, they'd talk. Then tomorrow, there would be actions taken. As soon as the knock sounded at the door, Rosie let out a long breath and opened the door.

"Come in." As soon as he was in the trailer, Cal just looked around. "Ruby has gone to get some sodas for us. I wasn't sure what you might want to drink, so there are beers in the fridge."

"Water is fine." Cal looked around again. "I don't know what you think I can do for you and your sister, Rosie. I mean, I'm just a bear shifter that hasn't had a great deal of luck in life. I can help her, but that might only be extending her life. And not in a good way."

"Give us time. That's all I ask for. She's all I have."

He nodded and then finally sat down. When her sister came back, she helped her bring in the sodas and other things that she'd not known she was out of. Cal helped with the bags, but when they were all standing in the kitchen of her camper, he just stood there holding onto the last two bags of groceries he'd brought in.

"This is Ruby, my sister. She's dying. I need you to fix her for me." He didn't stop staring at Ruby. "Are you all right? Say something."

"You're my mate." Ruby told him what she'd been saying all along, that she didn't have long to live. "You will now. I mean, my blood will heal you completely. Or at least until such time as I can change you. If that's what you want."

"I don't know you." He said he didn't know her either, but he didn't want her to die. "I don't know. This is all strange to me. I mean, we both know a lot of shifters, but none that…why are you really doing this? Do you think that it's going to be easy on you or something to have a mate around?"

He burst out laughing. And Rosie had a feeling that he was just as startled by the sound as they were. When he finally handed over the bags, he sat down. He made no effort to touch her sister, but he did stare at her.

"I'm a very old bear shifter, Ruby. I've been around…Christ, longer than a lot of vampires I know. That's where I was going. Am going. Tomorrow. I have a friend that is opening up a clinic where I'm going to be working at. Sort of get away from…I had a mate once. She died some time ago in childbirth. It happens sometimes but not often anymore. But I lost them both. I thought that I was going to be alone for the rest of my life and going to see Hamish, it would have—"

"Hamish Perry?" They both turned to look at her. "His name is Hamish Perry, isn't it? He contacted me through the travel board to come and help out with the clinic that he's opening for men and women to get help. Not just dried out, but—he's a vampire? Well, ain't that funny? Not really, but…we'll leave in the morning. The four of us. We'll eat now and then pack up to go."

"Wait, it's not that easy. I'm in the middle of an investigation. And so are you." She told him that she was leaving and he'd better make up his mind to go with them, or she'd hurt him. "You're really that bad assed, aren't you? All right. Let me make a few calls. And then talk to Hamish. How did you know that it was him?"

"How many people do you know that have the first name of Hamish?" Rosie was so happy that they both laughed. And when their dinner arrived, she was glad that she'd ordered a meat lovers for Joey. He was her best bud, and she loved the guy.

That night she discovered that her sister had already sold off her home and had gotten rid of all the things that she had. Whatever she couldn't sell had been donated, and they were well on their way to getting to Ohio.

Cal was going to have to work in the morning on transferring the information that he had, and she and her sister were going to get a start on packing up the camper. With being in one place for these last few months, she'd forgotten how long it took to break things down when she was ready to go. Rosie had gotten used to having her things out where she wanted them and was now regretting that decision. But she also knew that as soon as she was settled in Ohio, the same thing would happen, and she'd have to bitch at herself for letting things get so lax.

At midnight the two of them were in bed. Since it had been so late talking, Cal had decided to stay in the spare bedroom at the end of the camper. She and Ruby had ended up falling asleep, holding each other and crying for most of the night. It wasn't what she wanted, but Ruby was going to be all right, and she'd have her around for a bit longer. It was going to be all good.

By six-thirty, they were ready to go. Pulling out with Ruby behind her in her rental, she followed her to the rental place. By nine, they were on the road and having a good time. Rosie was glad for this time with her sister and was happy too when Cal decided that he'd take his truck home and meet them there. It was hard on the man, she could tell, but he seemed to understand that this was something that the two of them needed. And she did. More than she would have thought possible.

Chapter 1

Driving to Ohio wasn't nearly as boring as he thought it might have been. Of course, they were stopping every hour so that they could all rest up and he could spend time with Ruby. Christ, oh mighty, Cal couldn't believe his luck in finding his mate so late in his life. Life couldn't have been better than it was right now for him.

Cal knew that she'd been very ill of late. Cancer had a way of doing that to someone. But since he'd been able to give her some of his rich and old blood, she told him that she was feeling so much better. Calhoun could tell too. Each time she and her sister got out of the truck they were driving to pull the camper that Rosie had been living in while being a traveling nurse, she was laughing and having a much better time each time.

Pulling into the gas station right behind the camper, Calhoun was happy to see that the dog, Joey, Rosie's dog, had finally gotten over being jealous of him. He supposed that the dog knew in some way that Ruby was his mate and had been making sure that he wasn't going to hurt the woman. He didn't think that being a bear was all that reassuring for the dog either, but they were getting there. Rosie had been so accepting of him that he'd been surprised that the dog had been so hostile toward him at first. Then after he'd given Ruby some blood, the dog wouldn't allow him to go near her for the first few hours. Then he started to loosen up as they traveled together.

"Hello there, boy." Joey was as excited to see him as he was, Ruby. After petting him until he was calmer, he spoke to the dog again. "Come on. Let's go and see if we can find you something to munch on. I'm sure the women haven't been feeding you everything you want." It was a joke. The dog was spoilt rotten by the two women.

After getting gas and some snacks, the three of them decided to have dinner at the truck stop. Storing all the things that they'd gotten and putting Joey in the camper, the three of them entered the establishment and made their way to the restaurant.

"Don't let me forget Joey's dinner. He'll be upset with me if I come back smelling like a burger, and he didn't get one." Cal said he'd make sure that he got what he wanted. "Thank you. I'm going to have to put him on a diet after this. He's been eating like he's starved since we loaded up to go to Ohio."

Cal decided that when they were finished with dinner and found a place to camp for the night, he'd take the big dog out for a long run. He needed one too. They'd been driving from the coast in Florida to Ohio for three days now. Taking their time, too, he was glad the women allowed him to sleep in the spare bedroom in the camper so he'd not be too far from them when they set up. He was actually enjoying camping, especially with the huge rig that Rosie had.

She'd told Ruby and himself that she'd gotten it brand new two years ago. It made for easier traveling from one hospital to another as she was a traveling nurse. Since she was going to be living in it when not at work or traveling, she decided to go big or to go home. It was the biggest thing he'd ever seen, forty-three feet.

Not only did it have two full-sized bedrooms with

queen-sized beds in them, one at each end of the camper, but there were one and a half bathrooms for them to use. It had a larger kitchen than he had had in his apartment as well as a well-appointed outside kitchen that they used most nights while traveling. It was top of the line in all aspects of the sucker, and he'd never once felt cramped or shut in in the week they'd been traveling.

After eating, he slipped away with the dog's two burgers and got him out of the camper. The plan had been for him to go on a quick run at the campsite, but he just couldn't wait and decided to go out with the dog while the two women talked.

He felt bad for both of them. Only the little bit that he'd heard about their childhood after their parents had died, he wanted to find their aunt and show her what it meant by treating family nicely. After the elder woman had had a third stroke, Rosie and Ruby both decided that she could live in a nursing home for the later years of her life and not be a burden to them. That's all the woman had called his new family was a burden while growing up with her as their guardian.

Cal knew that they were both well off. Their parents had made sure that they had more than enough insurance for the girls when they were gone, and they'd only added to their wealth after getting out of college. Rosie had joined the service, and Ruby had gone on to get her doctorate in child psychology.

"Are you still traveling?" He smiled and told Hamish Perry, his dearest friend in the world and the one he was going to be helping out when they got to Ohio at the new clinic. *"I don't want to distract you while you're driving."*

"No. We only have to pull into our space for the next day or two then we'll travel straight through to get to you sometime late on Friday. The girls are still eating. Mostly I think they're just talking about me behind my back." He laughed with Hammy. *"You're not going to believe how much I'm enjoying this trip, Hammy. It was like when we were kids, and your grandparents took us on those long trips. Of course, back then, we were all terrified out of our minds of humans, but I'm finding that I like them all right now."*

"Yes, having a mate can make you all kinds of silly. I know that mine is for me. And Warren and Robin are as bad as we are finding time to sneak away from everyone." Cal asked him what he needed. *"Oh, yeah. I have three houses set up for the two of you to look at when you arrive. They'd been cleaned up, and the furnace and air conditioner has been checked out too. There are two smaller homes, both of them with two to three bedrooms in them, that you had me line up*

for Rosie. Is she still not going to live with you and Ruby?"

"She, and I really don't blame her for this. She wants to have a home settled under her feet and a place for her dog to roam around in the backyard. I honestly think it's more to do with her depression than anything. I did tell you there was trouble when we left Florida, didn't I?" Hammy said that he had. "I know then I've said this before, but had she not killed that man in the elevator with her when she did, he would have killed every newborn in the nursery as well as the staff that were there. Not to mention the rest of the people as he was leaving if he'd gotten that far. He meant business with several hundred rounds of ammo and guns like he had."*

"I can't imagine anyone wanting to kill a newborn, much less a bunch of staff members too, simply because his girlfriend had put his baby up for adoption without asking him first. It sounds to me like she made the correct decision." Cal agreed. "Anyway. Things are moving along with the clinic. Since we're funding it privately, there isn't nearly the red tape that we would have done."*

"I know about that too. The things you have to do to get one thing done in a hospital is a nightmare." Remembering that he had picked up Joey's ball in the camper, Cal began to toss it out into the grassy area where the trucks were parked. "You know, I've been hanging out with Joey,*

Rosie's dog. I never in all my life thought about getting a pet. Did you?"

"No. I mean, mostly because it would have taken so long for one to get used to me being a vampire, and secondly, I don't think I could have survived when it died. Over the decades, we lost enough friends to old age. Having a dog die on me would have sent me over the edge, I think. No, I never wanted a pet for those reasons and more."

After they finished speaking, the connection was closed. Making his way back to the restaurant, he noticed that the girls were gone, so he made his way to the camper instead. They were there, putting away the things they'd gotten earlier, and he was glad. The sooner they got on the road tonight and to their camping place, the sooner he could relax. Something that he was looking forward to when they left in a couple of days, Ruby was going to be riding with him.

The travel park was nice. Crowded but very well maintained. And there were trees, something that Rosie had been talking about since they were on the road to here. The couple running the place handed them all coupons that the local vendors gave them to hand out. Mostly it was to restaurants or a few bucks off something in their shop. He didn't mind supporting local businesses, but tonight he was simply too tired to think about going to town and shopping for a bottle of beer made by some local nearby.

"We will have to go to the grocery in the morning to get supplies for the next few days. I'm all for grilling out as much as we can. We've been good about getting things eaten up while we're camping, but as we're going to be here for a few days, we'll need some things to get us to the next spot and then on to Ohio. Also, if you have laundry, go get it tonight, and I'll put it in the washer when we go to bed. That way, we can dry it while we're gone in the morning." He noticed that while the camper belonged to Rosie, Ruby seemed to be in charge of getting the place cleaned up and tidy. Rosie wasn't a slob by any means, but she would get into her head with thoughts, and it would take her off of whatever she'd been doing. Cal told Rosie that he'd already brought it over. "Great. Thanks. Also, thanks for getting Joey out for some run time. I think he needed that."

"He seemed to have enjoyed it. I know that I did too. Also, he's going to need a new ball. The one we were playing with got smashed up by a trucker when he pulled out after I threw it." Rosie showed him where the dog's toys were, and he had to laugh. "Do you buy him a toy everywhere you go? He could open a doggie toy shop with all this."

"Yes, as a matter of fact, I do get him something when I have to travel. He'll play with it while we're traveling, then not much after that. His favorite toy is the big pig. He's had the thing since he was a pup." The dog seemed to understand that they were talking about him, and he pulled out the giant stuffed pig and showed it to him. "If I could find him another one, I would, but I've had no luck whatsoever in replacing it. As you can see from that thing, he'd about worn it completely out."

The rest of the evening was devoted to setting up and getting things put out so they could enjoy the next few days without having to go to much in the way of trouble. Cal told both women about what Hammy had told him. Then he asked Rosie if she was sure that she wanted to live in a home by herself.

"I do. That way, if I need to go away for a few weeks, I won't be upsetting your household. Besides, Joey and I will be fine on our own. After you two make me an aunt, I'll have plenty of people to hang out with." Neither he nor Ruby said a word but continued working on what they were doing. "Not that it matters, I guess. I was talking to Lander, Hammy or whatever he goes by, his wife. She said that they have company right now in the form of two teenagers, one of them pregnant."

"How old are they?" Cal had to think a minute when Ruby asked. "Fourteen and fifteen? That's much too young to have a child. Why they're just children themselves at that age. What happened?"

"Their father is a druggy, and when he didn't have enough money to pay his bill to his supplier, he let them have the oldest. Beth is her name. Missy is her sister." When Rosie handed him a glass of iced tea, she continued. "Lander said that they were staying with them. She was afraid of their parents coming around. I told her that if it would help, they could stay with me if they needed a place to hide out. Another reason for a home of my own. I might become a place for pregnant women to hide out. But I have to admit. I'd find their parents and kill them if it were up to me."

"That's what I was just thinking. Are they looking for the parents?" Rosie said that she'd not thought of asking them that. But she was sure that they were. Ruby snorted before continuing. "They'd better hope they find them before I do. That's just not right on so many levels that it pisses me off."

Cal was proud of his little warrior and decided

that he was going to have to step back when she was in the mood she was in now. Not that he was afraid of her, but he didn't want to piss her off when it came to him trying to save her when she seemed quite capable of saving all three of them. Cal was happy that he'd found his mate and more so that she was a hellion, much like how Hammy described the other two women in his family now.

~*~

Ruby liked camping a great deal. She hadn't thought of all the things that came with it and was glad that her sister was a seasoned camper. And that her camper seemed to have everything that was needed to make this trip not only enjoyable but easy too. Eating in didn't seem all that terrible as they were able to buy what they wanted and were able to cook it inside or out, depending on the weather or their needs. Also, she was glad for the time to get to know Cal.

He was a nice man. Full of humor, too, something that she'd only just realized. He and Rosie got along well too. Now that Joey trusted him, she did a bit more too. Ruby had read some place that animals knew a safe person when they met them. She didn't know if that was true or not, but she was going to believe it now, especially with Cal.

While the two of them, Rosie and Cal, seemed to have a great deal in common, she was surprised at how much the two of them had in common as well. He enjoyed camping as well, and they talked about that for hours. Mostly it was to do with the things they'd packed up versus what Rosie had packed. They were having fun with their list, and she'd not laughed so hard in a very long time. Even their jobs, him a psychiatrist and her a doctor of child psychiatrist, had a great deal in common too.

"Why child psychiatrist?" She asked him what he meant. "Why children and not adults? I mean, I see a lot of kids seeing a doctor for one reason or another, but I was wondering why you went into such a field."

"My upbringing. My parents were wonderful people. We had such an idyllic childhood growing up. Of course, there was money for us to do a lot of things that other children couldn't, but my parents never made us feel like we were super privileged. We had things growing up, but if we wanted something that they didn't think we'd take care of or need, then they made us pay for it ourselves. I'm betting that when Rosie bought this rig, as she calls it, she really had to make herself buy it by going over all the things that it would save her. Not just money on hotel bills and such but what she'd be able to do with it after she was finished being a nurse. Believe it or not, Rosie is a doctor. While she was in the service, they put her through college so that she could go to the front line when needed as a surgeon. She only worked as a nurse now because while it didn't pay as well, it afforded her more time off and less responsibility. A great deal less stress too. That's mostly why she's working as an RN. She's been under a lot of stress since our parents died."

"I would imagine that both of you have. What with you having cancer and having to deal with all the end of life things that would come with that." She looked to his left and saw something flying around the pole that held up the canopy. "Is there someone behind me?"

"I'm not sure that I'd label it as a someone. More like a…actually, I have no idea. But it seems bigger than the bugs we saw in Florida." He turned in his seat and then back around, telling her what it was. "Faerie? I don't know that I've ever encountered a faerie before. To be honest, I didn't know they were real at all."

"Oh, they're very real. There are thousands of them in any one place if you know how to look for them. Sometimes it's a matter of them allowing you to see them. That's the trick. This one seems to be vibrating with something to do with us. You, I would imagine, as I'm not one they usually seek out." She asked him how they were supposed to know what it wanted. "Put out your hand, and it will come to you if it's you he's looking for. It might be for me, but I don't—"

"Put out your and for it too. I haven't any idea, but I think that if anyone were to send a faerie, it would be that guy you and Rosie are going to see. No one knows that I'm coming there." He told her he'd contacted Hammy and let him know she was coming too. "Well, then, humor me."

They both put out their hands, and she hated that hers were shaking a bit. It was embarrassing how fearful she was of something so tiny. But almost as soon as Cal put out his hand, the little person landed on his outstretched palm and sat down. Getting up slowly so as not to startle the creature, she sat on Cal's lap when he offered it to her. Ruby marveled at the little woman that stood on his palm and missed what she was telling Cal.

She asked what was going on. "You were right. Hammy did send her to me. She has some information for us both, as well as Rosie. They wish to hire you as well to work for them." She said she'd not thought of getting a job since she was healthy again. "I didn't think you had, and while I know you have money, you don't need to work. I have a great deal of it saved up and stashed away."

"No, it's not the money. Not really. As we said before, we both had a great deal of insurance from our parents and grandparents when they passed on. Anything that would come from our aunt, the old bitty, is to go straight to the nursing home for her care." She then asked the faerie what her name was. "Oh, what a lovely name you have. I'm to understand that you get to pick them out for yourself? To be honest, Yum, I didn't believe there were such creatures until Cal told me. Not that it matters, but I am glad to make your acquaintance."

"The pleasure is all mine, Lady Ruby. I know a few faeries that are named after the beautiful gem too. They aren't as lovely as you are, however." When Cal cleared his throat, Yum turned to him. "I am to find a faerie for your mate, too, your lordship. Do you have any preference in mind when I go to find her one?"

"No, but I'd be happy too if you were to find one for Ruby's sister, Rosie as well. She also has a dog named Joey. He is a good dog but will need someone that will be able to be around him without fear. He is a canine, not a shifter." Yum told them both that she would find the perfect person for young Joey. However, she did suggest that a brownie for him might be a better choice as they are slightly bigger than a faerie. "Good idea. He loves to play fetch with a ball too. So keep that in mind when you look around."

After talking to the two of them for a few minutes, Yum took off to find her a faerie. She did wonder if she needed one, too, but her sister pulled in just as she was ready to ask Cal about it. She looked pissed off, and Rosie wondered what someone had said to her.

"You always think that the other person is the one that bothered me. Well, they did, but that's not the point. I am caustic when I'm having a bad day, you know." Ruby asked her what someone had pissed her off about. "Forever my hero. You know how much I love grocery shopping, right?"

"You hate it. We all know that. Cal hasn't ever shopped with you before, and I bet he knows that." He nodded and asked her again what had happened. "You have a bit of dirt on your blouse as well as your lip is swelling up the longer you stand here."

While Cal unearthed her first aid kit, she cleaned

her wounds up. When the police pulled into the lot, no lights or sirens going off, Ruby knew that it wasn't her sister's fault. They would have had all their lights running and their sirens going off. It was Cal that went out to talk to them when they got out of the camper.

"I didn't do anything. I was standing in the line for the deli when this woman hit the back of my legs with her cart, the chair kind that ran on battery, you know what I mean?" She said that she did. "I blew it off the first couple of times she did it. Me thinking that she didn't know how to run the fucker. Then she knocked into me so hard that I nearly fell into the meat counter. Probably would have if the man standing next to me hadn't grabbed me. The people behind the counter told her to behave, or she'd be banned again. She must be a wonderful person to be around — reminded me of our aunt when she didn't get her way."

"Entitled." Rosie nodded her head. "Yes, go on. What did she want? In front of you, no doubt."

"No, it was much worse than that. She was pissed off because of the handicapped placket that I have in the truck. I wasn't even parked in one of the handicapped spaces, even though I could have been with my military injuries. But she was pissed off that I had one. She told me and everyone else in the store that I was a freeloader and that I was probably sucking on the tit of society and milking the government for a handout. So I, letting my mouth get ahead of my brain, asked her if she had a thing about tits that give milk. I swear to you, Ruby, had I been able to do it over, I more than likely would have done the same thing. My filter is broken, as you know."

"Yes, honey, I know that. What happened then? I'm sure she was really putting up a fuss by then." Rosie smiled at her, and she knew whatever had happened was going to be epic. Then she asked her if she was humoring her. She was but chose to ignore that for now. "What did you do, Rosie?"

"I turned to her when she didn't say anything. And I was staring down the barrel of a Glock. A fucking Glock, Ruby. Out of instinct, I pulled out my own and pointed right at her head while hers was pointed to my chest. The man behind the counter, his name is Mr. Brown, he pulled his piece out too but aimed it at Ms. Downy. He started barking out orders to the employees around us. Getting the customers out was high on his list. Then he had them getting out the employees but for her to call the police too. I was all right with that, I guess, as I'd not pulled my gun first. But I wasn't going to be hurt either. I didn't want anyone hurt, really. So when the police arrived, the only people in the place were Ms. Downy, Mr. Brown and myself. All three of us pointing our guns at each other, mostly on the dumb bitch that had decided that I was sucking tits for some reason."

They were both laughing when the door opened. After the officer explained why he was there, the four of them sat around the living area and talked about the upcoming trial for Ms. Downy. The woman had pulled this kind of thing before, and now she was going to jail. Thanks wholly to Rosie for pressing charges on the old bat.

"I'll send an officer to see you in the morning if that's all right, Major. Thimble." Nodding at the officer, Rosie told him to call her by her first name. "If it's all right with you, ma'am, I want to respect your job for our country and for me and my family. It's men and women like you that makes me sleep better at night. So, thank you, Major."

After the officer left with assurances that Rosie would be there in the morning, they all settled down for the night. It was amazing to her what would embarrass Rosie. Being a Major in the service, something that very few knew about her sister, was something to be proud of.

But she'd never bring that part of her life up unless Rosie did. She wasn't stupid enough to think that her sister would cut her any slack about things.

Chapter 2

Cal was happy with what was going on around the campfire. It seemed like he'd been waiting for this time in his life just to spend it with Ruby. They'd been here for two days and decided to stay another two before leaving. He was glad about it. Chilling with his snacks, drinking a nice cola and having a great conversation with his new family was what life was all about. At least it was beginning to feel like that to him. It wasn't just the company and food either. But the intellect of the conversation and the people he was having it with as well.

Both women were smart. Also, Rosie had a sharp

sense of wit that had him testing his own sense of humor at times. Also, occasionally, at the start of this trip, his temper. Rosie could cut a person sharp enough that she could make you bleed. But now he's figured out that it was her defense mechanism in dealing with her depression. And right now, he could tell that it was terrible for the younger woman.

"You're thinking too hard, Calhoun. What the fuck are you stressing about so hard?" Rosie glared at him, something she'd been doing a lot today. "You think you know something, big guy? About me? You don't. No matter what you have in that little mind of yours, you don't know shit about me. And if you're invading my head like I know you can, you'd better get out of there and stay out." Ruby snorted before talking to her sister.

"What the hell is wrong with you? You've been acting like a bitch for the last couple of days. I'm not going to die, and you should be happy about that. Not only that, but I've found someone who loves me to pieces besides me. I'm sure there were times, not now, but usually, Cal likes you as well." Rosie stood up when Ruby did. "What is your beef? And I'm not going to be blown off again about your shitty mood."

"I'm not in a shitty mood." Pulling her jacket up

off her seat, Rosie started toward her truck. "I'm going to the store. If you think of something, message me. I'm not in the mood to talk to either one of you ass holes right now."

After she left, spraying rocks all over the camper as she left, he looked over at Ruby. If her expression was any indication, she was as confused as he was about the turn of events with her sister. When Ruby turned and looked at him, he saw something on her face that he'd never seen before. One that he didn't have any idea what it meant.

"She's upset. About something. Do you know?" Cal told her he'd made a promise to Rosie that he'd never invade her mind unless it became necessary. "You don't think this is necessary? She's being a royal bitch right now, and I'm worried about her. What is wrong with her?"

"I can't look, honey. I can't break a promise to her. You have to admit that this isn't life or death, whatever is going on with her. And that's what I promised her." He would do it if she insisted, but he really didn't want to. "But, if you'd allow it, I'll have someone else look and see what's bothering her, like my friend, Hammy. He'll do it for you. He's been better at it since before he was able to — I did tell you he was a vamp, didn't I? Well, he can do it better than anyone I've ever met."

"Because he's a vampire?" Cal nodded, then told her that he'd been around even longer than he'd been. "Do I want to know how long you've been around? I mean, is it something that — You know what? Never mind. I'll just think of you being my age. Perhaps a few years older. Cal? Will you stay with me until I'm old and gray?"

"I would if you were to ever get old and gray. Honey, Ruby, you're going to be as beautiful in a thousand years as you are now. You'll never get old, never gray, nor will you ever be sick. Also, I'm not sure why you'd worry about this, but you won't ever gain a pound except if you were to have our child. Even then, you'll not keep it on but be my most beautiful mother ever created. And I will worship — "

"Enough. You're being sappy." She started pacing back and forth, and Cal watched as not only her breasts bobbed a little, but she had the finest — "What are you staring at? Are you looking at my ass right now? My boobs?"

"Yes. Yes, I am." He laughed. More than likely more than he should have. If her face was any indication.

"You're beautiful. What can I say? I love looking at you. Imagining what you look like under that shirt. About what you look like without anything on? Am I being too sappy? I could go into more detail about what I'm thinking about all the time. Like, are your nipples pink or rose-colored? Are they as full as they look? Will they fill my hands when I lift them up to suckle at them?"

She simply stared at him. Cal wasn't sure if he'd gone too far or if he'd pushed her into something that he promised her that he'd not. He'd told her that them making love, when and if it happened, was entirely up to her. But he'd suggested things to her that he'd been thinking about since meeting her.

"You've been thinking about that? How long?" He told her the truth. She started pacing again, talking under her breath. He was only able to catch a word or two. Cal was reasonably sure that he was either being called a pervert or he was the sexiest man in the world. Deciding right then and there, he wasn't going to piss Ruby or her sister off again. He reached out to Hammy.

After explaining what had happened and asking him if he'd look, Hammy popped to their campsite instead of answering him. After one of his great bear-like hugs, the two of them started talking all over each other.

When Ruby poked him, he turned to introduce the two most important people in his life. Hammy hugged Ruby, welcoming her to his kiss. That took some explaining too.

"It's the leader of a group. In this case, vampires. Also, just recently, I've been named king of all of our kind, and my lovely mate is queen. My kind, I mean." Hammy looked at him. "I'm babbling. Lander has gone to see Rosie. You read up on her? Wow, she's brilliant."

"No, I've not looked into her. I don't know that she'd appreciate that much. But as for the two of them being brilliant? Yes, they both are. And she's not going to be happy about your wife, I'm assuming, popping up at the grocery store where she's at." Hammy said that she wasn't going to hurt her. "No. I'd think that you, that is, if you're worrying, you should be worrying about your wife. My sister is a mean person. And she won't care— Oh my gosh. I know what it is. She's unhappy because I suggested to her that she needs to settle down in one place and do what she was born to do. Be a doctor. That's it."

When Ruby went into the camper to start dinner, she told them Cal looked at Hammy. He asked him what he'd found out. With a shake of his head, the two of them sat down in the chairs around the fire and leaned back.

He wanted, just a little to know what he'd found out, and a big part of him didn't think he should know.

"I'm not allowed to even peek into her head. Lander said that she wanted to talk to your new sister by herself. Something about needing a doctor at Highlander. Which, I think I told you, is named for Lander's father. It's a good location and set up. But not just to help people to dry out but to get the resources they'll need to get back up on their feet. Something that her dad never got the chance to do. Mostly because he was so ill all the time that he didn't have anyone to lean on." Cal told him that he was sorry. "I am too. I didn't ever meet him. However, being around as long as we have, we've seen this sort of thing happen to both women and men. And there hasn't been anyone around to help them out."

"Yes. My father died that way as well. Remember when my brother was killed? I'm not blaming it on Jamie or anything, but he did take a great many chances with being around humans all the time. Then when one of them turned on him, he didn't have the support system in place so that he could hide out until things were quiet, and it got him killed. That made my dad take to drinking. It wasn't known back then the effects of alcohol on shifters, but it did do a number on my father's liver and kidneys since he refused to shift to help himself heal. I think towards the end, had he been willing to shift, it wouldn't have done him much good. His liver, from not taking care of himself, had gotten too bad." Hammy told him how sorry he was again for his loss. "I appreciate that, Ham. More than you can imagine. You've always been such a good friend to me and my family."

They didn't talk about Rosie or what was needed of her again. When Ruby called them both into supper, he wondered if either of the other two women was going to join them. Noticing that the table was set for three, he and Hammy washed up and joined Ruby at the table. She'd made them thick pork chops with all the trimmings. Cal asked about Rosie.

"She was talking to Lander when I called her. I don't know what about, but when I spoke to my sister a little while ago, she said she might need me to come and bail her out of jail." She looked at Hammy. "I guess your wife is pushy. But Rosie is very good at saying no to anything she doesn't want to do and sticking to it. Trust me on that one." Cal asked if she had any idea if they were coming back to the camper. "Rosie said that she would be home late. She had a few things that she needed to look into."

The rest of the meal was the three of them talking about camping. Just as they were having a slice of cake — carrot, his favorite, Lander, showed up. She seemed upset, but he wasn't sure as he'd never met the woman before. Enjoying the cake and hot tea, the four of them ended up outside again around the fire. Rosie still hadn't shown up, but no one seemed worried, so he tried very hard not to worry either.

"You mentioned that your sister was in the service. What did she do, if I can ask?" Cal wasn't sure that Ruby was going to answer Hammy, but she finally did. "Special Forces? I didn't know they had surgeons in that group of servicemen."

"She was called a battalion surgeon. And they do. Mostly for things that might occur while they're out on assignment, but they do have them." Hammy asked about her training. "Rosie is brilliant. However, not to hear her talk about herself. When she committed to the service, she was already a doctor of some fame at the hospital where she worked. She claimed that the reason that she joined the service was to get her college paid for. But I don't believe that's entirely it. To be honest, I don't know a great deal about my sister's time in the service. We went our separate ways in a great many things, yet we kept close when it mattered. Rosie suffers from depression more than anyone I've ever met, to be honest. She can hide it quite well for a long time then it will come crashing down on her all at once. Like today, I think."

"You said you thought you'd figured it out." Ruby nodded at Lander, telling her what she'd thought. "That's not it. I mean, a little of it is about you, but that was just the topper for her. She's upset that she might be losing you. I know that the two of you know some shifters, but the only ones that your sister has had much in the way of contact with aren't what I would call usual. Rosie believes Cal will be taking time away from the two of you getting together. He wouldn't. But she didn't want to hear that from me."

"You argued with her then?" Lander nodded but didn't look like she was happy, as she might well have been arguing with someone else. "She was upset when you and she were in the store. Rosie said she'd call me back later tonight when she was in a better frame of mind. Can you tell me what else is upsetting her? While I believe you might be right? I can't see her walking away from Cal rather than confronting him about her concerns. What happened between the two of you?"

~*~

Rosie sat on the seat at the table by the ice cream shop and watched the trees sway back and forth. It was helpful for her depression sometimes to concentrate on things of nature around her. Twice now, she'd been interrupted by a small creature, a faerie, he told her, but she told him to go away. She didn't want anyone around.

He was persistent, however, and stayed nearby her no matter what she threatened him with. Finally, giving up on trying to be alone, which honestly never worked out very well for her before, she waved the little guy to her.

"Miss? I do have things to talk to you about. Also, I'd like to offer to get you something to eat. You've not eaten in a good long time, and it will make you ill if you were to skip any more meals." She said that she was an immortal thanks to Mr. Bear Asshole. "You've said that before. I'm assuming that you're referring to Lord Calhoun?"

"Do you know any other? Never mind. I'm sure you know a lot of bear shifters." Turning to look at the little man as he sat on the picnic table she was sitting at. "Why do you think it's important that you be with me? I think it's because Bear Ass can't tell what I'm doing from where he is, or there might be something else? Which is it?"

"I am to be your companion." Rosie asked if she looked as if she needed a companion. "No, my lady. You look like you could, if you'd not mind me saying, take on an entire pip of my kind and not have any trouble. However, we'd never harm one such as you are."

"One such as me? What exactly does that mean? Because I know for a fact that before Bear Ass came along and his vampire friend, I was just a regular old human being with a lot going on." He said that she was so much more than that now. "Why? Because he said it should be, and it's the way that things are to go."

"No, my lady. It's because you've been given a bit of magic from the queen of vampires." Rosie remembered that other woman mentioning something about queens and vampires. She asked the little man if he had a name. "I do, my lady. My name is Doyle. And as for the magic that she gave you, I doubt she would have been able to control what you were to receive when she touched you. You are quite powerful in your own right. As your sister will be once she is able to touch the fine queen as well."

"And after she has sex with Bear Ass." His little face turned a nice shade of blue. Why? She didn't have any idea, but it was sort of cute on him. "All right. So you're to hang out with me for some reason. And while you're hanging out, I'm going to be working. Tell me, how is that supposed to work for you? Because I'm not going to spend all my time explaining why I have this little person hanging on my shoulder or wherever you might be to everyone that I come in contact with. I don't enjoy explaining myself under normal circumstances. I certainly haven't any idea how to explain you."

"No human will be able to see me unless you allow it. Also, shifters and other nonhumans usually know better than to ask about a faerie or whatever else you might be hanging around with, as you call it." He landed on her leg. "The queen has said that the two of you argued, and that upset her. Is there something that I can do for you to make it better between you and Lady Lander?"

"No. Not unless you can tell me why she's bugging the shit out of me to be a doctor at the clinic when I know for a fact that she has several lined up already." Doyle smiled at her, showing sharp teeth that even though they were tiny, she was sure they could cause some real damage if necessary. Then he told her what he knew. "I guess I can see that, but I'm not sure how happy I'm going to be just staying in one place all the time. I love being able to travel with my job. I can pick up the phone anywhere and talk to my sister, and she can do the same with me. I don't need to be up her ass to know that I like being around her all the time."

"Up her ass? I don't…oh my goodness, my lady." Doyle seemed to have taken that literally and fell back on his ass. His shocked expression made her laugh a little. It took Rosie three tries before she could tell him what she'd meant because she was laughing so hard. "Oh yes. I can…my goodness, you are descriptive, aren't you, my lady? But 'tis not the same as being there for each other. I miss some of my sisters and brothers that were born when I was. It's good to see them at fall harvest and spring planting."

When he didn't say anything more, she looked back to the trees. Her heart was aching today. Why, she couldn't fathom, but it did have a mind, it seemed, of its own when she was down like she was right now. Glancing at Doyle, she started talking as she watched the trees again.

"Being a doctor means something different to me than it does to most who take the oath. While I was in the service and out on a mission, it was difficult for me to make the calls that were necessary when one of the team members was killed. My primary job was to ensure the people that we'd sometimes go after were given good care, but even that wouldn't turn out the way that I'd like for it to." He told her that he was sorry. "As am I. I can't think being a clinical doctor for the place they're opening up will be much different. Men and women who are on their last days coming in to die will be hard on me. Especially over a short amount of time that they might well have left. Do you understand what I'm saying to you?"

"Yes, you think they will only come to the place when they're dying, close to it at any rate. Or even to dry out from one thing or another? I don't know about that, my lady. Do you think they'll not improve once they are there?" She nodded, telling Doyle that some people that abuse their bodies with one kind of substance or another wouldn't ever believe that they're going to die. "I guess I have seen that too, my lady. They think they have a handle on their illness when in reality, they don't. Some never think that they're in the wrong about themselves. Yes, I can see where that would be upsetting to see the same people time and time again to get better and then fall off the wagon, as humans say."

"I think that's why I enjoyed being an emergency

room nurse all this time. It's fast-paced usually, and it's seldom that I would see the same patient more than a couple of times while I was working there." She leaned back on the table he was on now. "I would be able to see my sister more, I know that. But I don't want to be settling for her and not for myself. I'm a grown assed woman, and I know myself better than she does."

That caused her to laugh again when she had to explain to Doyle why she thought it was so funny. They'd only just been talking about people thinking they knew themselves better than others. But she did have a point, Rosie thought. She didn't want to be the third wheel in her sister's new life.

"They'll have children and a life. If I hang around, she'll want to include me in all their plans. Again, I'm old enough to not do that if I don't want to, but she'd insist, and then Cal would, and I'd feel like I have to go to keep the peace. Does that make sense?" He said that it did. That he understood what she was saying exactly. "Thank you. I just have to figure out a way to explain to my sister that I don't want to be hanging around when they get all lovey-dovey around each other, and I feel stupid. I've already seen the way that he looks at her. Like she's a big piece of juicy steak, and he can't wait to have a portion of it."

"That is quite descriptive, my lady." She laughed again when his face turned blue. She asked him about it. "I am a blue night flower. There aren't many around anymore, and since that is the flower I was made from, my embarrassment turns a lovely — or so I'm told — blue."

"So you are born in flowers?" He explained to her that all worker faeries were born that way. "By you saying that, I'm assuming that there are other kinds of faeries born in different ways. And you mentioned pip. I'm assuming that's what a group of you are called."

"It is. Yes, a pip. But as for being different kinds of faeries, there are as many of them as there are snowflakes in the winter months. Oh my, yes, there are so many. I was born, as I said to a blue night flower. There were hundreds of us born the day that I was. However, over the decades, many, actually, most have died. Now that there are so few of the flowers left, there aren't as many of my kind around any longer." Rosie asked him to tell her about himself. "I used to be a worker faerie like all the others. Then when I reached one hundred years old, a young faerie, even at that age, I was given the choice of continuing on as a worker or I could be something else. Still to do with the earth and all its glory but not having to toil so hard daily. I decided that I wished to be a morning dew faerie. I would go around with my new magic and touch the blooms of flowers with dew to wake them up. Oh, that is such a lovely sight, to see them unfolding their petals and leaves to be able to greet the sun each day. My flowers were in a cemetery that I watched over with thousands of other faeries."

It was then that he showed her his arm. She reached down to pick him up, and he held out what was left of his appendage to her. He explained how he'd been hurt, nearly killed one day by a child who had been out looking for trouble.

"This child, he had a net that he was using to scare off others like me. You see, children, when they are born with just a bit of magic, can see us when they're close. He not only saw us but tormented all the little creatures that were there to work with, keeping the park beautiful for those that came to grieve. This child had been trying to capture the butterflies that were in the park of the dead." Doyle moved to sit closer to her when she put her hand on the table for him. "I was gathering up the dead. He'd killed so many by tearing off their wings and squashing them. He was harming them for no reason either when he captured me in the net with some others. Being around the area for so long, I knew to have something in which to cut some of the dying flowers off. Well, I hurriedly used it to cut through the netting to free the others. However, a butterfly had been caught up in the thing and was sure to die without my help. Once I had her cut loose, I was caught in the terrible creature's hand."

Doyle was missing his hand and most of his forearm. As he continued with his story, telling her how the child had tried to pull his wings off as well, she looked at the little man. There were scars all along his cheek and forehead. She could see then, too, under closer inspection, that he'd also lost his eye. It was a small wonder that he could get around. He'd been hurt so badly. But Rosie had a feeling that what she was seeing wasn't all the damage that he'd taken that day.

"Brownies came to rescue me, thankfully. Once I was able to cut my way free of his grip, I was taken to the queen of the earth to be saved. There wasn't much of me to be saved, I will admit, but she did help me to heal. After that, until this day, I've been hanging around the castle with the queen until such time as I decided to die. Then I saw you." Rosie cocked her head at the man and decided that they were perfectly matched for each other. "You were so sad when I came here. It was my job, you see, to bring you several faeries that you could choose from to be with you for all time. But the moment I saw you, I felt a touch to my heart that I've not felt in a great many years. A need to help someone that is much like I am. Sick of the earth and the people that occupy it. Was I right in that?"

"You were." He told her too that if she didn't want to be seen with such a damaged creature like him, he'd willingly go back to the castle and live. Shaking her head even before she spoke, Rosie knew that if she had wanted to turn him away, which she did not, he wouldn't last until the end of the day. He'd take the rejection as hard as she would have and end his own life. "You and I are a pair, Doyle. I wish for you to be not just my companion but my friend as well."

She decided that she needed to get back to the camper; however, on the way, she was going to stop and get herself something to eat. While she didn't normally care for fast food, right now, she thought she could eat several large orders of French fries and not think a thing about it. After telling Doyle what she was going to get, he asked if she could get him some too.

The hamburger was hot and juicy. The fries were so crisp she could hear them snap when she bit into one of them. Doyle had some of the strawberry milkshake she ordered, and he enjoyed the lettuce off her sandwich. As they sat in the parking lot, enjoying their meal, she told him about the house she was supposed to be living in when they reached Ohio.

"It's a lovely house, my lady." Again she asked him just to call her Rosie, but he just ignored her. Like he had every other time she'd said it. "There is a nice large back yard that Joey will enjoy. He'll have a brownie with him for all time. It was suggested as he is a dog, it might be better if he were to have someone a little larger than I am. Also, they'll be able to communicate with each other as well. It will be good for the two of them, I think."

"He's a lot calmer than he used to be when I first got him. He'd only been a puppy back then. Now that he's older, I can leave him in the camper in his crate so he doesn't get himself into things he shouldn't be." Doyle asked her if it was necessary for him to be in the crate. "With the brownie with him, I haven't any idea. But when Joey is bored, that's when he gets into things. I don't like to do that to him. He loves to roam around the place playing with his toys, but he also makes big messes too. What do you think will happen when there is someone with him?"

"He'll be calmer still. No longer bored either if that is what you wish for the brownie to do with him. Also, he will be able to take him out doors to use the bathroom. I was told that was something that he'd need as well." Rosie said that he does well without having an accident in the camper. "The brownie will be able to keep an eye on him while outside. That will make Joey happier too. Also, the two of them together will be good for your neighbors. I have heard that one of your neighbors in the park has a barking dog. All hours of the night, I was told."

"Yes. We've only been there two days now, and I want to go over and tell them to not let their puppy stay outside all night. The poor thing gets scared. I've even been tempted to kidnap the little guy and make sure he's warm at night in the camper." Doyle told her it was sad he had to stay out in the night air. "I suppose it wouldn't be so bad for him if he were to have something out there to sleep on. But he doesn't even have a rug to lay on. Anyway, I've been giving him treats to try and keep him company when I go out at night to take a walk if Joey needs it."

"You've got a kind heart, my lady. Very kind indeed." They finished off their dinner, and she drove them back to the camper. Being careful of her usual manic driving, she pulled into the camp spot gently so as not to knock Doyle around too much. As soon as they were out of the truck, Doyle made his way to the man sitting with Cal. She supposed it was Hammy, the great vampire that she'd been hearing all about.

"You have a nice night?" Shrugging, Rosie sat on the other chair that was around the fire. "You don't like Cal all that much, do you?"

"I don't know that I'd say I don't like him. My sister seems to. I guess he's all right." She turned and grinned at the other man. "I will admit I've been having a good time at your expense by calling you names. But a girl has to have some fun, don't you think? Nah, I'd say you were all right, too. Pushy as fuck, like that wife of yours, but I can take care of myself." She laid her gun on her lap to sort of prove to them that she was able to care for herself. "I've been thinking about shit, and that usually gets me into deep shit. But I will hang around the clinic for a few days before I make a decision about staying on as a doctor. I won't be pressured."

"No, it's doubtful that anyone would try that again." She nodded and tossed another log into the flames. Hammy introduced himself to her. "I hope we can work well together. We all want this to work. Especially my wife."

"Yeah, the queen of your kind." He nodded and smiled at her. "Do you think that'll have people running into the place knowing that there are vamp's working there? Or are we downplaying that for a while?"

"Downplaying. Most in town know that I'm a vampire, and I've figured out over the years that so long as there is enough money going around and no one is dying, they'll pretty much let you do anything you want. Within reason. What about you?" She asked Hammy what he meant. "Do you think you can downplay your role in working for us as magical as you are?"

"That's what Doyle said. That I'm magical. How do you know that?" He told her that she practically glows with it. "Well, I guess we'll see just how much juice I have in my fingers. But again, I will not be pressured. We do this my way, or I go. It's as simple as that."

"I agree." He put out his hand, and she hesitated a few seconds before asking him if it was safe for her to touch him. "I don't know. Lander said that you got zapped from her. So did your sister, by the way. But not anything like what happened between Lander and my sister. Time will tell, don't you think?" She nodded and put her much smaller hand into his.

Almost as if her body was waiting for the small shake before it zapped her, Rosie felt her body being torn apart. Not painfully, but enough to know that she was being given something that she'd never had before. Before she could pull her hand away from Hammy's, she felt herself flying through that air and hitting something hard and stationary behind her. Then nothing.

Chapter 3

Ruby wasn't sure how Cal was going to react to her news when she rode with him for the last part of their journey. She hadn't ever met anyone like him and doubted she ever would again. But it had been her sister who had finally had to sit her down and tell her what was going on. Never would she have believed that someone could fall in love so quickly and so readily as she had with Cal.

"Why are you making him wait on you sleeping with him?" Ruby told Rosie that she wasn't ready for that yet. "Oh really? You two could cause a fire the way that you look at each other sometimes. And frankly, Doyle and I are taking bets on whether or not you'll be knocked up by the time we get to his home."

"It's not that bad." But it really was. Every time she caught herself looking at the man, she could feel her body soften and warm up. Just the thought of him touching her was enough to send her into a combustible fire of lust and need. "He's not even kissed me yet."

"Then kiss him." She was helping prepare dinner for the three of them while they talked about her lack of relationship with Call. "You're wasting a good set of lips if you ask me. It's not like you to be shy around someone."

"I'm not being shy. I'm being cautious. I don't know if this is real or not." Rosie snorted at her then so did Joey. "You're teaching that dog some terrible manners, Rosie. I swear he acts just like you do."

"Thanks." After explaining that it wasn't meant to be a compliment, her sister laughed. "I'm just saying that if you ever get the opportunity to jump his bones, warn me so I can put some reinforcements under your end of the camper. I don't want to be caught up in the sucker when you two knock it off its set up."

Rosie had always been able to say whatever she was thinking. She supposed that was something that she'd be used to by now. But she wasn't. It would make her giggle, sometimes laugh loudly what Rosie would say to her, but with this, she wasn't ready to show her how embarrassed she was about her comments.

They were having salad with grilled steak over it for lunch. Then for dinner, they were headed to one of the restaurants in town. Warren and Robin, along with Hamish and Lander, were going to meet them there. She was both excited and terrified out of her ever-loving mind to get together with them. Rosie was going too with Doyle as her date. It had taken her nearly two hours to convince her sister that they all wanted her there as well. She had also explained what she was feeling about being their fifth wheel. Ruby was glad that was cleared up now too.

"Let me ask you something." Ruby told Rosie to be nice. She was nervous. "I'm never nice, so you need to get over that. I was going to ask you what mom or dad would think about Cal? Or the others? I have an idea what Dad would say. Mom, too, but you tell me what you think."

"Dad would be just like you. Asking me why I've not been laid as yet." Rosie laughed. Of late, she had noticed that Rosie was laughing a good deal more than before. "Mom would smack dad on the arm, tell him to behave himself, then she'd be taking me upstairs to look at her wedding gown to see if it would fit me well enough to use."

"Will you?" Ruby asked her what she meant. "Use mom's dress? I know where it is. I also, just yesterday, had the butler pull it out of the chest and have it cleaned for you. The veil too."

"You did not." Rosie tossed a carrot at Joey, who caught it in midair and then promptly spit it out. He wasn't a healthy eating dog, she supposed. "Why would you—you really didn't do that, did you?"

"I did. It'll also be shipped to your new home when it's ready. I don't want you to have any excuses for putting things off for the two of you. I like Bear Ass. A great deal. He's got a great sense of humor. He's not too stupid, and he's good at giving as much as he is taking from me. I like that about him." She asked her again to stop calling him Bear Ass. "Nope. Not going to happen. It's our way of telling the world that we like each other. Besides, I think he enjoys it. Shows him I'm all bad ass and shit."

When Cal joined them in the camper, he kissed them both. Her on the mouth and Rosie on the cheek. It was as natural as anything else that was going on. Cal even referred to her as his sister when he was talking to someone. When he sat at the dining room table, she waited for him to tell her he'd been joking about his love for her.

"Will you calm down?" Rosie kissed her, too, then worked on putting the large salads in the bowl. "I swear to you, Bear Ass, she is forever waiting on the other shoe to drop. What were you able to find out about the houses. You were headed that way with Hammy, right?"

"I took pictures of both homes. I really like yours, Rosie. You couldn't have a better home than the one they got you. Joey has an entirely fenced-in backyard. Lots of shade, so he won't ever be too hot. Also, there is a spring on the back that fresh water comes from it. That'll keep him hydrated. There are five bedrooms in it, five and a half baths." He handed her sister his phone as he continued. "The kitchen is a cook's dream. Doyle went with me, and he's made sure that all the equipment in it is ready and waiting for you. Laundry on the second floor as well as room for the gym if you still want to put it in." When Rosie handed her the phone, she looked the pictures over as Cal explained what she was seeing. "The front yard is nice. The sidewalk will lead you to downtown. Your neighbors are a good distance away from your home on either side, and there is an open lot across from you."

"Did you take care of our family home, too, like we asked?" Cal pulled her into his arms and held her there as he told her that all the furniture had been packed up and was sitting in trucks to come to their homes. "Thank you for that. When we went there last night, I couldn't believe how out of date things were. You think that selling it will be an issue?"

"While I was there this morning coordinating the moving of the furniture, there were several people already there asking to see the inside of the place. The realtor Hammy suggested answered all their questions but for the price." Rosie asked why they didn't tell them the price. "I'm so glad that you asked. Dave seems to think, now that he's gone over the place, that you're not asking enough for it. He told me he'd call you two later tonight, but he thinks you should double the price and perhaps even go a bit higher. He told me that you can always go down, but once you sell it, there is no raising the price."

"That's going to be nearly a million dollars, Bear Ass. How the hell does he think that will bring that much money?" Cal told Rosie that the house had a long history.

"It does. Little of it is any good. When our parents were alive, they thought about selling it as well. If they hadn't died when they did, they would have, I believe. But not nearly for a million dollars."

"I think we should do it." Ruby looked at Cal and then at her sister. "You and I both know that we don't need the money. But to settle this estate up and get the thing off our books would be wonderful. I know for a fact that last year's taxes were a great deal more than we had been told. Not only that, but I'm to understand that the place needs a new furnace as well as central air put in it. Then there is the kitchen."

"It's been taken care of." Ruby asked Cal what he meant. "I mean that while I was there, Yum came to see me and asked what we were doing with the house. I told him what I knew. That the house isn't anything that either of you want to live in because of the memories and that you wanted a younger family to live in it. He said that he thought that it would be too expensive of a place to have to remodel. He said that in no time, he and the other faeries that were in the yard and beyond could have it picture perfect."

Taking his phone from him, she sorted through the pictures as he then explained what they'd done to the house. With Rosie over her shoulder, they both looked in awe at the house that just last night was in shambles as well as the yard looking like it was a field for cows. It was in such poor shape.

"The roof looks new. That was going to cost us a great deal if it had to be replaced." The two of them pointed out things that had been something that needed to be repaired, and that was now finished. The walls were a beautiful white color, and all the heavy curtains, something that her mother had liked, were gone. The place was now bright sunshine and earth tones shining on the walls from the stained glass windows.

Cal put the salads on the table while they continued to look through the pictures. They talked about what it would have taken for the house to look this good if not for the faeries. Cal explained that they had wanted to do something for the two of them because they'd been so generous with their time and letting them help with the camping needs.

"All we did was give them a place they could pack their things while we traveled with them." Cal told Rosie that it was all they had wanted. "Well, I think having them around is going to make me lazy. But I do love them to pieces. And Joey, he's loving having someone around him all the time too. And look. Did you see this? They got him a pink pig."

Ruby loved the dog as much as Rose did and had cried tears of happiness when he'd been given the giant pink pig. The dog had run around for hours with it in his mouth. Showing it to everyone but not allowing them to touch it until he was ready. And when he'd laid down, he had even shared it with the faeries to allow them to rest on it, too, when he did.

After lunch, they sat outside again. It was supposed to rain later in the evening, and they could all feel it. Tomorrow they were headed out again. Since it was the last couple of days traveling, they had been packing up the camper again so that they could get out early if they wanted. Ruby was looking forward to riding with Cal and talking to him on the last leg of their trip.

Taking a walk around the park where they were staying, she noticed that everyone seemed to know Joey and Cal. She knew they'd spent a great deal of time in the park fields with the dog, chasing the ball and throwing it, but not that they'd been so friendly too. Mildly jealous, Ruby took Cal's hand when they had two women walk up to ask Cal if he could move something for them.

"I can do that." He kissed the back of her hand.

"I want you ladies to meet my future wife. As soon as we get to Ohio, we're going to be getting married and having Ruby make me the happiest man on earth."

The two women seemed to be in a huff about her being with Cal, and he told her that he'd been trying to avoid them all week. It was funny to her that Cal seemed to be embarrassed at their obvious flirting style, and she was sure that it made her love him all the more. Then it hit her. She was in love with Calhoun.

~*~

Cal was glad to be finished driving. They had pulled into the driveway of his and Ruby's new home about twenty minutes ago, and he was unpacking their things from the back end of his truck. Rosie had gone on to her home with the camper and her truck and said she'd see them in a couple of days. Her plan was to clean out the camper from top to bottom and then winterize it for the cold weather. It surprised him every time he learned something new about campers.

"There are several messages here for you." He took them from Ruby after getting a kiss. "You keep that up, and we're never going to get the truck unloaded. And I don't know about you, but I'm going to need a nap soon. I feel like I've been run over several times in the last few hours."

He did too. They'd had to come through a couple of smaller towns when coming here, and it had been nerve-racking for everyone. While Rosie was doing the driving of the truck and camper, he had been assigned to drive ahead of her to make sure she could get in and out of not just a place to have lunch but gas stations too. Another thing that he'd learned about. Not just the length of the camper you have to worry about but the height of them too. It had been scary close when he'd found one that could accommodate the rig.

But they were home now. He and Ruby had toured the house when they'd first pulled in, and now they were just wanting to get things squared away and finished up so that they could get a head start on their lives. They'd even been able to call the local grocery store on the way in and have a large order delivered so they'd have food in the house for tomorrow. He was looking forward to having a steady floor under his feet, a shower he could take his time in and a place he could stretch out in a bed. The camper did afford him all that. The floor didn't move all that much, but the bed was something that he missed. Being over six and a half feet tall didn't fit well on a regular queen-sized bed.

Once Ruby left him to go up and shower and go to bed, he settled in his new office and set up his computer. Hammy had done him a solid in getting the house looking like they'd lived there forever, but there were things that even he couldn't do for him, like setting up a place for him to be able to do business at home.

It was nearing midnight when his cell phone rang. He didn't recognize the number that came up, so he didn't answer it. But he did check the phone a few minutes later when it told him that he had a voice message. He'd not even realized that he'd had voice mail set up until he had to put in a pin for it. It took him four tries, his last try to get it right so that he could get the message left for him.

"My name is William Talbot. You got my kids. Janet and I want them back" It took him a moment longer than the man wanted, apparently to tell him that he didn't know what he was talking about before he started screaming at him. "Don't even tell me that you don't have them. I know better. I want them back to me right now, or I'm calling the police on your fucking ass. Where are they?"

"If they're your children, I would think that you, of all people, would know where they are. Or that you should know, at least. I haven't any idea what you're talking about." The man was still talking, cursing, really, when he hung up on him. Almost as soon as he closed the connection, it was ringing again. This time he knew the caller. It was Rosie.

"I've been called out to the clinic. Someone is giving birth. I wouldn't have bothered you, but I haven't any idea where the stupid place is." He laughed a little and asked her if it was the Talbot girl. "Yeah. I guess. I didn't get anything, but a fifteen-year-old was in labor. How did you know?"

"Her father just called me demanding that I give him back his kids. I'll meet you over there. I don't want you to be caught off guard while handling the baby if he happens to show up." She told him that was a good idea and said she'd meet him there if he had the address. "I don't, but I know where it is. Have Doyle tell you where it is. I'm sure he'll know."

When she simply hung up the phone, he smiled. Rosie wasn't one for long conversations when she had the information that she needed. Leaving a note for Ruby, he made his way to the truck. He was thrilled that he'd had time to clean it up before he had to use it again.

Getting there proved to be easier than he had thought it would have been. Rosie's truck was already there, so he made his way in, hoping he'd not have any trouble. Without someone to vouch for him made him a little nervous. But he shouldn't have worried at all. Not only did they know he was coming in, there was a police presence because they'd been getting threatening calls from Talbot for a couple of days now.

He didn't bother going to the curtained-off area where he was told the girl was. He heard Rosie barking out orders about things that she was going to need. When the officer approached him after introducing himself to him, he asked Cal if he'd contacted Hamish.

"I never thought of it, but I suppose one of us should." The cop, no more than a kid, he thought, asked if he'd do it. "Of course. Are you, by chance, afraid of him?"

It had been a joke, but Officer Hershey said that he was more afraid of his wife. She was scary when she was upset. He told the officer that he should work really hard on not upsetting the other woman, and he nodded so hard that it looked like his head might fall off soon if he didn't quit. Contacting Hammy was a piece of cake.

"The clinic called here a few minutes ago. I had no idea they were going to call Rosie. Nor did I think they knew how to get in touch with her." Cal wondered if the faeries might

have told them. *"Could be. I haven't any idea. We're leaving the house now and bringing the younger one with us. Missy has been staying with us while her sister was on bed rest there. It seemed better for the girl to be able to get round the clock care."*

"Rosie is here. She called me because she didn't have an address. I don't know that she was upset with the call, but I don't know her moods that well yet. I'd say to you to be prepared for her temper. It's a good one too." Hammy told him he'd charm her. *"Yeah? I don't know that she'll take that any better than she has being roped into a job she wasn't sure she was taking yet. Just giving you a heads up."*

It wasn't twenty minutes before Hammy and his little family were there. He knew Beth and Rosie were in one of the operating rooms now. While he wasn't sure what was going on with the baby, he'd seen the staff racing to the closed-off curtain right before Hammy arrived. Lander had gone to the end of the building where they were after hugging him and asking him to keep an eye on Missy. The kid seemed all right to him.

Missy was only fourteen years old, he'd been told. But she had what his momma used to call an old look to herself. An old soul. She didn't seem all that upset about being awakened in the middle of the night. Nor did she seem terribly upset about her sister giving birth. However, she did tell Hammy to remind Lander of her promise to Beth.

"She knows. And as she's told you both before, she doesn't like it. For that matter, I don't like it either." When Cal started to ask what was going on, Hammy simply shook his head a little. He knew he'd tell him later, but for now, he was making reassurance to the younger sister. "Are you hungry? I know that there is food in this place. What it might be, I've no idea. But I can get you something." Missy looked at him before answering Hammy.

"I'm not hungry. My sister wants to die having this baby. Twins, they told her when she got here. And she's made them all promise not to save her life with magic or anything else to save her life. She's got some. So do I, but she said she didn't want to live if they had to use up their powers to make it happen." She leaned her head on his shoulder. "I think she doesn't want to live anyway. I do, but Beth said she's sick and tired of life. I don't know how that is since we're just kids, but I know she's hurting because of what our father did to her. Not just one time either."

"I'd like to have a little talk with that father of

yours. Perhaps even end his life." Missy looked up at him and then resumed leaning on his shoulder. When she whispered that she wished someone would have killed him long ago, Cal looked at Hammy before speaking to Missy again. "You really don't want that, do you honey?"

"I really do. Both of them. He gave us away whenever he didn't have any money. Even if he had the money, he and our mother would watch men taking us. They made a game out of it, too, a lot of times. Like when one of us screamed, he'd be owed a hundred dollars. He'd beat Beth and I a lot so that we could hold out in screaming to make it worth his while. I never screamed for him. Not even when he put a gun to my head. I'd rather of died than have him making money off of what they did to us. But Beth, she's delicate. She would scream and scream all the time they were raping her. I know it's not right to hate somebody, especially your parents, but I wish they'd fall into a deep hole and rot there." She looked up at him again. "I don't think she'll try to get better. She told me the other night that she was broken. Too broken to be a person anymore."

Cal stood up to go and talk to the young girl. Perhaps this wasn't the best of times, but he had to get to her before she gave birth. Because he knew as surely as he was walking down the long hallway that Beth would will herself to die. Like so many other mistreated women and men that he'd met in his lifetime.

Just as he was getting to the end of the hall and figuring out where he needed to head, he saw Rosie and Lander. They were talking, and it looked as if Rosie was comforting Lander. His heart broke for them both. He knew that he was too late to save the young girl. When someone took his hand into theirs, he looked down at Missy.

"She told me that I was to help whoever takes the babies. I can name them too, but I don't know what I'd do to make that happen." He said there were people there to help her. "Do you think we'll be put out on the streets, Mr. Cal? I mean, nobody wants to be saddled with twin babies and a fourteen-year-old without anything to our names." Cal got down on his knees in front of the little girl. He could see that she'd been crying, tears still streaming down her face. "I don't know what I'm going to do now. Do you?"

"I'll take the three of you in as my own, honey. You never have to worry about that again." He hoped that he'd be able to. That Hammy and Lander hadn't already made plans to keep them. Not to mention, he'd never thought to ask Ruby. "You'll come and stay with us, you and the babies. I promise you, with all that I am, that you will never be subject to the kind of treatment you got from your parents again."

He hugged Missy when she started crying and held her to his chest, his own heart breaking for the young woman. When Rosie and Lander came towards him, he did mouth the question if the girl had lived, and it was the shake of her head that had him leaning his face into the neck of Missy to show her how hurt he was as well. Christ, she was only a child and had been through more than most adults had in their entire life.

When Lander said her name, Missy turned to look at her. All Cal wanted to do was to run from the building, holding her close to his heart where she was now. The small push at his mind had him confused for a moment then he heard from Ruby.

"I just heard from Rosie. Those poor little girls." He told her that he wanted to bring them all home with him. *"You do it. And if anyone there gives you any shit, you let me know, and I'll make sure they see who's in charge. Those poor babies. I'm on my way now, Cal. Oh, I love you so much."*

"I love you too, my heart. I, in all my lifetimes, have *never hurt as much as I do right now for a near stranger. But we'll be good parents to them all. I know it."* She told him that she knew that too. *"I'll have to talk to Hammy and Lander. I love you, Ruby."*

"I'm so sorry for your loss, little one. I tried my best to help her, but she just didn't make it." He watched as Missy stared at Rosie as she spoke. "Lander said that the two of you were very close and that she had mentioned to you that she wished to pass. I'm so profoundly sorry. I don't know what I'd do if I lost my little sister." Missy hugged Rosie and told her that it was going to be all right.

"I'm sorry as well, Missy. It breaks my — would you like to see your sister?" She shook her head at Lander, then nodded. "You don't need to see her if it will upset you more. The babies are fine. A baby girl and a baby boy. They're in a different room right now, so if you want to — "

"I do want to see them, but not right now. I want to see Bethy, if that's all right, then I want to go home with Mr. Cal. He said that he'd protect me and my babies. My sister's babies." Lander looked confused, but Rosie started laughing as she turned and walked behind the closed door. "I think he'll do as good a job as you would, Ms. Lander, but like you were telling Bethy and I. You needed to find us a sitter while you and Mr. Hamish rested."

"We'll talk about it later if you want." Cal didn't know what was going on, but he was thinking that he might well have overstepped his bounds in this. It wasn't until Hammy came to stand with him that he felt a little better. He still didn't know what was going on, but he was willing to bet that they'd talk about this very soon. He hoped so.

Chapter 4

Ruby didn't know all that much about babies. She did treat small children, but she wasn't prepared for someone so tiny as this one and her brother were. Missy came to sit with her and asked her if she needed help.

"I think I might." Missy showed her how to hold the little girl and then how to give her the bottle that had been prepared for her. She looked at Missy as the baby took to the bottle like she'd never eaten before. "I'm to understand that you're to name your niece and nephew. I thought that since the funeral is the day after tomorrow, that would give someone plenty of time to get their birth certificates filled out and filed. Lander said that you were being very closed mouth about the names."

"I've been thinking." Ruby nodded as they both watched as the baby enjoyed her bottle. "Bethy told me that she wanted me to stay with them. To make sure that they knew all about her when they got old enough. She's left me with too much to do, I think. I've been looking on the internet, and nobody wants to adopt a girl like me. Not only being fourteen but someone that is damaged. They called it that too. Damaged. I guess I am. So was Bethy. But it wasn't our fault."

"No, it wasn't. And I want you to know that if anyone calls you that again, you let me know. I'll make sure they know the meaning of the word damaged. And you're right, Missy, none of this was either of your faults. You were dealt a bad hand in life, and Cal and I are going to make sure that you never have to suffer like this again. I'm sorry for your sister passing, Missy, but I think it was somewhat selfish of her to have left you with the care of these wonderful children of hers." Missy said that her sister said that she was sorry about that as well. "You two must have spoken a great deal about the children and what might happen to them. Did she tell you why she didn't want to live?"

It had never been in her mind to sugar coat the

things children would go through that would bring them to her. Sometimes she'd be reprimanded about her ways, but mostly the children and most of the parents would trust her more by getting to the root of things. Missy picked up the little boy and held him like a pro. Ruby found herself to be a little jealous of her in that.

"Can I tell you what happened to us?" Ruby was thinking that she didn't want to know but said that she did to Missy. "The night that we ran away, it wasn't the first time that our parents sold us off. He made a game of it. But that night, he…the man that raped Bethy promised her that he was going to steal her away from our parents and have her tied to the bed for the rest of her life. Then he cut her."

"I saw the scars on her body. Some of them were never treated." Missy rocked the little boy as she sat there quietly. "You were cut up as well, weren't you, Missy?"

"Yes. He said he was marking us so that no one would ever want us but him." Ruby wanted to pick her up and hold her until someone went to kill that man and this child's parents. "When he found out that she was going to have a baby, he paid my dad a lot of money to be the first to have sex with her child. That's when Bethy and I ran away. It took me a long time to get over the fact that a grown man would want to defile a baby. That's what the internet called it. Defile. Anyway, once we were able to escape, we stayed close to home. Our thinking was that he'd think that we'd ran away. Being close, too, helped us to be able to sneak into the house and get money and food when they were gone. It was scary that. But we managed to get some needed things when they were out."

"May I ask you why Beth didn't want to live?" Missy rocked the baby back and forth for a long time. Ruby didn't think she was going to answer her, but almost as soon as she was ready to tell her that she didn't want to know, the little girl started to talk. Her voice was low and full of pain.

"Bethy has always been tender about things. She'd cry at movies and books sometimes. Even when she found us a kitten that was hurt, she cried for days when it passed away from its injuries. That's when she told me that she didn't want to go on with life." Putting the little boy in the bed that had been put together just this morning, she sat in the window seat and looked out over the back yard. "We talked a great deal about what we were going to do with the baby—we didn't know there were two of them when it was born. She hoped it was a little boy, both of us thinking that that man, his name is Todd Perkins, wouldn't want him. But we just didn't know. One night, while I was digging through the dumpster at one of the grocery stores around town, I found some baby clothing. I don't know why they were in there, but I showed them to Bethy. I think that was when we both realized that we'd never be able to raise a baby on our own. The price, you see, for the little sleeper thing was nearly twenty dollars."

She'd purchased clothing for the babies this morning so that they'd have something to wear home. It had been a shock at the prices of things. Diapers too. They were outrageously overpriced, she thought. Not that they couldn't afford whatever they needed, but that didn't make her feel any better about the prices. Missy said that she had the names for the babies picked out too.

"I'd like to name the little girl Elizabeth Anna after my sister. And Nathan Patrick for my nephew. If that's all right with you." Ruby told her that she loved both names. "It took me a little while to name Nathan. I wanted him to have a good strong name but also to be something that no one would make fun of him about. That seemed like a good one. My grannie's maiden name was Patrick, so that was easy enough."

"I think they're both good names. Will you call Elizabeth Bethy?" She said that she thought Liz might be a better nick name. "Whatever you want, Missy. They're both really good names."

Nodding, she sat there for a little while longer while Liz finally fell asleep. Both of them were sharing a crib right now as they didn't seem to want to be parted for very long. Once they were together, they seemed to need to touch one another, too, and that would make them rest easier as well. Ruby let Rosie know what their names were so that she could finish up their paperwork for the adoption.

They had hired a nurse to come in and stay with the babies for the first few days they were home. Ruby didn't know anything about raising a baby, much less two of them. And she was going to try her best to make sure that Missy was involved in all decision making with them. Missy mentioned that Lander nor Hamish had seemed upset about her and Cal had wanted to adopt the babies.

"I think once they thought about how much they'd have to do with them, with both of them being vampires, it was better just to let someone that could be there for them all the time raise them. I don't know a lot about vampires, but I'm sure that there is a lot more awake time than either of them had thought of when it came to taking care of them." Missy said that was what they'd told her. "I thought as much. So, my dear. How about the two of us go and pick up my sister, and we head into town to get you some much-needed clothing. It'll be winter soon, just about a month from now, and you'll need a coat and warm boots to wear. Also, we'll need to get you enrolled in school."

They were headed into town about an hour later. Rosie was glad to go as she needed to get some things for her new home. Joey needed an extra bed so that he'd have one on the deck when he was out, as well as one in his bedroom. Missy thought it was funny that the dog had his own room.

"He has a lot of toys." Ruby laughed as Rosie explained to Missy how she picked him up a toy everywhere she went. "You should come over sometime and look at what he's accumulated. He favors one animal more than any, and 'I'm so glad that someone was able to get him a replacement for his pig. It was beginning to lose a great deal of his stuffing every time he played with it. But he loves having a home and a yard. When I let him out when I get home, it's hard for me to get him to come into the house again."

"I've never had a dog. Not even a cat or anything like that." Rosie explained to Missy that she'd not either until her doctor suggested that she get her someone that she could take walks with. "Does that work? I mean, getting you out of the house to see other people? Your sister told me that I needed to get out of the house too. But I'm afraid of seeing my parents and them taking me again."

"You have a faerie, don't you?" Missy told Rosie that she had a boy one called Jim. "Good name. When you go out, make sure you take him with you. That way, you won't be alone, even if you're walking Joey or your own dog. Trust me when I tell you, they'll never let anyone get close enough to harm you, honey. They're there for that very reason. I mean to be your friend, too, but they'll protect you with their lives."

"I don't want anyone to die for me." Ruby told her that they could call on a lot of others to save her, and very few, if any, would be harmed. "I'll think about it. It's scary just thinking about him being out there, just waiting for me to get to someplace where he can snatch me up."

"You do know that the police and a lot of other

people are looking for him, don't you? I mean, your parents aren't going to be free for very long. And I know that Cal is out there searching for them too. He's been looking into some other things that they've been up to that will keep them in jail for a long time." They entered the department store that was in an open mall kind of setting. As soon as Rosie spotted the yellow dress in the window display, she wanted Missy to try it on. "This is so summery I want to start the season all over. But I think if we were to get it in a bit of a larger size, you'd be able to wear it next year too."

The two of them wandered off, and Rosie looked in the baby department. Not that she thought the children needed any more clothing, but it was fun to look at the cute thanksgiving and Christmas outfits that they had out. She was just putting the one she liked for Nathan in the cart when Lander suddenly appeared in front of her.

"Don't scream." Ruby said she was all right now. "Good. I need for you to be extra careful for the next few minutes. Janet was spotted about five minutes ago in a store on the first floor of this place. I have two faeries on her now and a lot more out looking for William. Just so you know, Janet looks like someone that has been using drugs for a long time, and it's catching up with her."

"Now that you say that, I haven't any idea what neither of them looks like." Lander described the woman to her. "Okay, that will make it easy to find her. I'm surprised that she's not been tossed out of here."

"Me either. But she is being watched. I didn't know that your sister carries. Has she done that for a while now?" Ruby said she'd done is since she'd been in the service. "Good. She might be just the person we need to have confront the two of them. Before I forget, the paperwork has been filed for the kids. All three of them are now adopted by you and Cal. We did change the name of Missy to Meyer, but she doesn't have to call herself that if she doesn't want to. Your wedding licenses have been filed as well. Just in the event someone wants to know how you adopted the three of them without being married. I hope that's all right."

"Whatever it takes to keep them, I'm all for it." Lander and she walked in the direction that Rosie and Missy had gone. It was important for her to make sure they were all right. "The nanny showed up last night and took over night duties. I'm not sure how she feels about the faeries watching her, but I don't care. They keep a good eye on them, and that's more important to me than making sure her feelings aren't hurt."

"She has a clean background as well as—Ruby, that's Janet standing over there next to the cookie store." She looked in that direction and took in as many details as she could about the woman. Janet looked like a homeless person. Her hair, an indistinct brownish color, was standing up on end. Even from where they were standing, she could see that her clothing was filthy as well as her shoes looked worse for wear. When she turned to look around, Ruby watched as she stole a handful of cookies from the counter and then slid away. It wasn't three minutes before she saw William too. "He's cleaned up a little better than she is, at least. I know for a fact that he's been run out of two stores since they got here. I've spoken to Rosie to tell her where they are. She told me that she and Missy are headed this way. I think I see them coming this way now."

It was them. Missy had a bag from the store they were in clutched in her hand, and Rosie looked like she was searching for someone while seemingly keeping Missy busy with pointing out things that were on the hangers around them. Hopefully, she was keeping an eye out for the Talbots.

They decided to get lunch then. It wasn't hard to convince Missy to join them. She was very excited about the jeans and shirts that she'd picked out. Even the coat, a little too big, was something that Ruby thought she might well have picked out for herself. After their orders were taken and salads were brought, Missy looked at the three of them and laughed.

"While I appreciate you guys trying to keep me safe, I'd really like it better if you were to tell me when they're around. I saw my mother twice now and my father coming out of the men's room with stolen pants on. The reason I knew they were stolen is because he had the tags still on them." It was Rosie that started laughing first, then she and Lander joined her. "Now that we know just where they are, do we call the police? Or wait for one of the other men to come and get them?"

"Robin, I don't know if you've met her yet or not, but she's working with the police to capture them. She is claiming to have seen them stealing something from one of the higher-end stores." Lander pointed to the long hall of the mall, and they all turned to see the police taking Janet in custody." Just as she was being escorted out of the building, William was being detained by the Feds. "He is being arrested on Federal charges stemming from the death of your sister. He took her across state lines in order to sell her. Your name wasn't mentioned for the simple reason you're living here now, and there isn't any point in bringing your name into this or that of the babies to keep you out of the papers."

"Thank you." Missy picked at her salad while sitting with them. "What's going to happen if they get out of jail? I mean, there is a possibility, right?"

"Not that I think it will happen. But if it does, they'll die." No one said a word as Rosie said what would happen to Missy's parents if they did happen to get out of jail. She looked around the table as if surprised by the silence. "What? You don't think I could do it? Missy is my niece now. And so are the other two. I will, if need be, go to prison for the rest of my life if I have to. You are safe now, Missy. I swear to you on my mother's heart."

~*~

Cal had everything done by the time Ruby and Missy returned home. A delivery of some of his things from his home had arrived, and he put them where he thought they needed to go. Not that he wouldn't move them again if necessary, but they weren't sitting in the hallway now, and that was all right with him.

Also, he'd been able to unearth some of the things that had been his mother's, too, that he wanted in his home. Then next week, his sister, whom he'd not seen in about a hundred years, was coming to visit. Cal didn't know if he was thrilled about that or not. Danny could be a handful sometimes.

Ruby came home without Missy an hour later. He was sort of surprised by that as he'd been able to get her desk and computer set up for her. Also, the babies were with the nanny, and it occurred to him that it was only him and Ruby in the house. As soon as he realized they were alone, he started to have the most impure thoughts in his head that he wasn't sure where they were coming from. It had been nearly a month now of them sort of living together, and he wanted his wife in the worse kind of way. He went in search of her.

Finding her in the kitchen, he heard her humming to herself. Asking him what he wanted for dinner, Cal said the first thing that popped into his head. He said he wanted her. The plate she had in her hand shattered to the floor as she turned slowly and looked at him.

"Me?" he smiled at her and told Ruby that was all he wanted for the rest of his life. "Me? I mean, seriously, you want me."

"You sound surprised. I must be losing my touch if you don't think that I've been making passes at you for the last few days. I mean, really." Ruby looked at the mess on the floor and then back up at him. "I don't care if the house is covered from top to bottom in crap. I'll take you right here on the countertop if you give me the word."

"All right." She moved toward him, putting her hands out so he could help her up on the counter. "I'm not sure that the front door is locked up, but I'm ready anytime you are."

Instead of answering her, he took her body to his as he pulled her body closer to his. Willing her to be naked, he, too, shed his clothing and knew that whatever happened next, if she turned him down, he was going to sob like a small child. When Ruby wrapped her legs around his waist and then locked them at his hips, he had to take several deep breaths before he could do anything more than stand there.

"You smell like honey to me." Ruby giggled and asked him if that was a bear thing. "I suppose it is. But you do smell wonderfully good."

Kissing her again, he pulled her arms from behind his head and laid them on the counter so they held her body up just the way he wanted her. Her body was more beautiful than he thought it would be.

Her skin was supple. Tan lines from lying out

on the beach in Florida made him want to lick a path along the different skin tones. Her breasts were full, and her nipples were hard peaks that seemed to beg him to suckle at them. But not yet. He had more exploring to do. Even when she sighed, he delighted in the way her muscles played along her ribs and tantalized him until he couldn't take much more.

Running his hand up and down her ribs had her making little sounds, soft sighs, moans and even a little catch in her breath. Kissing her navel, he made his way down to her pussy, her scent called to him with each breath he took. Squeezing her thighs and then her calves, he could feel the tone of her muscles. Running, he knew that she and her sister ran daily, and it showed in every curve of her legs and ankles. Taking her foot into his hands, Cal massaged her foot, her toes curled around his fingers. Bringing one to his mouth, he kissed each toe as he made his way back up her leg until he was at her hip again.

"Please, you're making me crazy with need, Cal." He told her that he wanted to explore her. "I need you. Very badly."

"I'm getting there." He licked his way over her pussy, then slid his tongue into her slit. Tasting her, the flood of cream filled his mouth as she held onto his head and held her to him. Suckling at her clit, holding it in his mouth while he played with it with his tongue, he slid his fingers into her sheath and felt her body adjust to him as he slid in and out of her.

Eating her was a dream come true for him. No better meal, even dessert, ever gave him such satisfaction as this did. Having his mate and her giving him all that she was couldn't have been better had he planned it.

Cal feasted on her pussy. Drank deeply of her cream. Each time she begged him to stop, he'd slid his fingers into her, fucking her this way so that she'd come down his throat. He ate at her for what seemed like hours. It wasn't until she jerked his head up by a handful of his hair that he thought she'd finally had enough. He was only just beginning.

Pulling her body to his so that she hung just off the counter, he slid his cock deep inside of her. The scream that she released was like music to his ears. Picking her up so that she clung to him, Cal pressed her against the wall and took her slowly. Fucking her in and out while she held tightly onto his shoulders while he held her.

"More." He told her that he wasn't ready to give her more yet. But she begged him so nicely and prettily that he found himself fucking her harder, holding her bottom closer to his groin so that he could feel each stroke that he impaled her with his cock.

Her scream of release startled him. It was loud, animalistic, like that he felt his bear roll along his skin. It felt like his beast wanted to mark his mate too. Nip at her flesh, mark her so that any who saw her, smelled her would know that she was his. Cal felt himself biting into Ruby's tender flesh even as he realized that he might well hurt her.

Hot blood filled his mouth. Her scream of a second and then third climax was more than he could have hoped for. It was then that his own body released. Not just his cock but every part of him emptied into Ruby, making her his for all time.

Even as he fucked her, his body going through the motions of taking her even though he knew there was nothing left inside of him. Still, he held onto her. Keeping her close, telling her over and over how much he loved her and needed her.

When he woke, not even realizing that he'd passed out, Cal found himself in his bed with Ruby lying next to him. Not moving any part of him but his eyes, he looked around the room until he could think that it was much later than he thought it was. The room was dark, and the light blanket over the two of them had him smiling slightly, wondering at whoever had moved them had at least covered them up.

Almost afraid to reach out to see who it might have been, he was startled awake again by Ruby curling around him. The room was lighter this time, yet he was still at a loss as to who might have carried their naked asses up to the bed room and put them in bed.

"I swear to you I didn't look no more than twice at your pretty little mate before I put her in your bed. At least, I hope it was your bed." He asked Daniel how he'd gotten him up there. "Now, that is going to be something you have to talk to Hammy about. We were coming over to see you when we walked into—the kitchen was a mess, by the way. So he called in a cleaning crew to not just clean up but to put the room to rights. Man, when you take your mate, you don't do it by half measures, do you?"

"Thanks for taking care of us, but don't mention it again. Not unless you want me to tell Ruby what you said about her naked body." He asked him if he'd really do that. "Absolutely. I will do it without ever thinking twice about what she will do to you either."

"Christ. You're not at all nice, are you?" Cal moved a little and moaned at how sore he was. "There has been some development since the two of you have been out. Not that you've been down but a few hours, but you know humans. They can fuck up a wet dream with time to spare. I've met my niece, by the way. She's a cutie. She is not very trusting, but after hearing how she ended up in your care, I don't blame her much. And those babies are around the most adorable little things I've ever seen. Anyway, Janet, her mother, is dead. I don't know a great deal about detoxing, but that's what happened to her. She had a stroke that took her life while they were trying to get her cleaned up. The father, William, he's taken it hard and his threatening every agency known to the humans blaming everyone for her death. He seems to think she should have been left alone and not bothered her about her drug use. The fucker said that he needed her when he got his daughters back. Neither of them are aware of Beth nor her children."

"Thank you for that. What are you doing that has you in the know? Not that I care, but I was just wondering." Daniel said he'd been looking for him and stopped at the police station to see if they knew where he was. He'd touched a few minds when he figured it out about the kids he has too. "Three of them, Daniel. A little boy and two of the prettiest little girls ever."

Cal met his brother at Hammy's after waking up Ruby. Rosie showed up about ten minutes before he left, and they were going to take care of some things at the clinic. Cal was just happy that he was able to get out of the house without too much going on, and Daniel hugged him tighter than he thought Hammy did when he first moved here. It felt to him like things were finally falling into place. At least for him and Ruby.

Chapter 5

William didn't understand how they could convict a man who had just lost his wife. And since it was their fault in the first place, blaming it on her wasn't very nice either. So what if she was a druggy? It wasn't anyone's business but their own. Looking down at the notes in front of him that this court-appointed attorney had given him, he wondered what the man would say to him when he figured out he could neither read nor write. That was his wife's job too.

"Mr. Talbot, are you listening to the proceedings that are going on here today?" He said he was trying to but wasn't understanding much of it. "What part do you not understand?"

"How come I'm being here in this courtroom when some bastard stole my children from me, and he's out running around like that's okay. My wife is dead now, and I got to sit here in this courtroom and listen to all this crap because some shit head decided that I'm a menace to the community." The judge told him to watch his language. "I'm trying to do that. You already told me to do that before. But like I was saying, I lost my wife, my kids and—hell, I mean heck, I was going to be a granddaddy too. I ain't seen hide nor hair of my kids since they were taken from me."

"Your honor, I can clear some things up for Mr. Talbot if you'll allow me to." The judge asked the woman who she was. "Special Forces Major Rose Thimble, Medical Physician for the United States Armed Forces. I've been helping with the cases that Mr. Talbot is talking about. And as such, I've been briefed on all manners of this case so that I could answer any questions that you or the defendant might have pertaining to this case. If that is all right with you, your honor."

"Yes, Major. Please clear this up. I haven't been able to review any of the files I've been given because this was last minute. This will, I'm assuming, make things run more smoothly for all parties in this case." They swore the woman in and then asked her if she was going to be telling the truth. Once she said yes, they sat her down in the chair next to the judge. "Now. Which part are you familiar with, Major?"

"All of it. If you'd not mind, I'm going to refer to my notes so that I get the names correct." He told her to go ahead, and William felt like she was sucking up for some reason. "Mr. Talbot had two daughters, Melissa Talbot, aged fourteen and Elizabeth Talbot, aged fifteen. The grandchildren that he was referring to were given birth five days ago, and Ms. Elizabeth, unfortunately, passed away while giving birth to a set of twins. The physician on duty was myself, and I did everything I could to save her. However, she was much too young to be giving birth, not to mention her overall mental health and physical health were too poor for her to withstand the trauma that she endured in getting pregnant in the first place."

"Bullshit. There isn't any way that she died." The woman asked the judge something then the bailiff handed him a sheet of paper. "I can't read this. What the hell is it?"

"Her death certificate is the top copy. The other

two certified papers are the birth certificates of her two infants. A boy and a girl. Both healthy and have been put into foster care along with Melissa Talbot." William said that he wanted his children and grandchildren. "No."

He waited for her to explain herself, but she didn't say anything more than just no. William started to stand but realized that he was chained to the floor as well as his hands were chained together. Sitting back down, he asked her what she was talking about.

"In addition to the death of his eldest daughter, Mr. Talbot is also directly blamed for the rape and sodomy of his underaged daughters. He prostituted his daughters for monetary gain as well as drugs for both him and his now deceased wife, Janet Talbot."

"She's lying." The judge asked him what she might be lying about. "I don't know. Everything, I guess, like my family being dead. I know that my daughter isn't dead, nor is my wife. There is no way that she'd leave me like this. Especially since I'm making plans for getting out of here soon. I don't know how either one of them can be dead unless she had something to do with it. And don't think I won't be getting my grandkids back either. They're mine, and I have plans for them kids. Missy too. She's gonna earn her keep from now on too."

"Earn their keep? They're just infants. Your other two children are minors too. I don't know what kind of job you think they can hold down being just babies. Unless you have other plans for them. Do you?" He told her never mind. He was going to work it out. "You mean by selling them off to the highest bidder? That's not going to work, I'm afraid. Your buyer, Mr. Todd Perkins, has been arrested just yesterday for armed robbery. He told the police that you were going to sell him your daughter's baby so that he could be the one — let me check my notes here — oh yes. To pop their cherry. He needed the money, he told them, because you were a man true to your word, and you'd let him have at the child if he came up with the money."

"I'm supposing that you took that from him too." The woman said that he'd broken the law by robbing the bank. "You people just want everyone to be just as lowly as they can be, don't you? It's hard to make a living if you won't leave us alone, you know. So what if he was going to have him a bit of fun with the baby. I'm not saying that it was going to be my baby but so what? It's not like the kid would be able to tell on him or anything."

William could feel all eyes on him at that second. Looking around the room, he asked what the hell they were looking at? A few of them said that he was a sick bastard. It made him giggle a bit to think that someone was actually thinking he was sick about something so stupid as babies.

"Mr. Talbot, I think we've all heard enough of your crimes as well as your opinion on them." He said good and stood up, putting out his hands to have them unchanged. "You will be remanded over to a higher court, at which time you will be tried for the list of crimes against you. This is the part where I usually tell people that I hope god has mercy on their souls, but I'm of the opinion that you don't have one. Neither you nor that wife of yours could be considered humans by the way that you've treated your own children."

"How the hell was I supposed to have any kind of food in my belly? Answer me that. Not to mention a little spending money. Those babies? When are you gonna turn them over to me? They're my grandchildren, and I need to get on the ball and get me some money coming in." The judge stood up and made his way out of the room. William looked at the young woman that had been blabbing everything about him. "You there? What kind of time line should I be expecting my family back to me. You're a woman, ain't you? When are you going to reunite them with me?"

"I hope you rot in hell. You piece of fucking slime." He told her that wasn't answering his question. "Never. They're in a good home with good people, and you'll never see them again. And if you do happen to get out of jail? Well, I surely hope that someone takes your life nice and slowly so that you suffer in ways that those wonderful girls did at your hand."

William didn't understand what was going on with people today. They trussed him up like he was some kind of bad guy, putting him in the van again. There was also the matter of someone killing his wife. He wasn't so upset about Beth being dead. She was getting too old for him to sell anyways. Not that he could do much with that Missy bitch. He'd never seen a kid fight so hard at trying to fight off a man in all his life. Twice he'd had to give their money back when his daughter, who he thought would want him to have the best of the best, had beaten up a paying customer so badly that they'd had to be rushed to the hospital. Kids had no respect for their parents nowadays.

"Mr. Talbot." He looked around the van where he was chained down and didn't see anyone at first. Then as this man dressed all in black appeared before him, he could only stare at him. Christ, he was the scariest thing he'd ever laid two eyeballs on. "Mr. Talbot, I'm here to end your life."

"Why? You heard what that judge said. I was going to be put in a bigger jail, not killed off. I didn't do anything wrong if you think on it." He said that he had murdered his daughter by selling her off to men that raped her. "So? What would you have done had it been your little one? Christ, holy mites, it's like I was telling that man in there. I have to make a living, don't I? And she should have been happy to be helping us out as her family. It's not like she didn't get a bit of food when she rested up a bit. 'Course, it wasn't as much as she wanted. I couldn't allow her to get fat or anything. Who'd want her then? Nobody, that's who. Nah, you don't want to kill me off. You can, if you'd not mind, let me go. That'd suit me a bit better."

William felt the wind move over his body, like a nice cool breeze that would give you a lift if it was too hot outside. Looking out the window of the van, he felt dizzy and sort of sickly to his belly. Looking around for the man again, he couldn't see hide or hair of him.

"Hey? Somebody up there? Where did that guy go? I think this other feller made me sick or ill." William was feeling a bit off. He wasn't entirely sure what was making him feel off, but he decided to rest his head against the wall to gather up some much-needed strength. "Hey? I'm not feeling so good. That other man, he said that he was gonna kill me. I think he might have hurt me instead. You have to help me."

It was getting more difficult for him to keep his eyes open. He didn't know what was happening to him, but he didn't feel very good. Looking down at his feet, thinking he'd stand up if he wasn't chained, he saw a puddle of dark liquid pooling under him. There was something shiny there too.

Moving his feet around until he could get a better look at the thing, he noticed that his shoes, the ones they'd given him in the jail, were all pink and red now. Surely that couldn't be blood. He'd not been anywhere where he'd cut himself. Lifting his head up again when someone said his name, he tried to tell them that he'd been hurt by the man that had been in the van with him.

"There hasn't been anyone in here—what the hell have you done to yourself? Christ, you're bleeding out. Call an ambulance." The people in the van were moving too fast for him to keep up with, and it was making him sick. He could make out a few words like blood and knife.

Also, that someone was going to jail for giving him a way out of prison.

William opened his eyes when he felt movement under him. Not sure where he was going, he could see lights flashing by him one at a time while people were screaming about transformation, whatever that meant. Then there was a face, large as any head he'd ever seen, right there in front of him.

"Mr. Talbot? Why did you do this?" He asked what had been done to him. "You've cut your arteries in your thighs. We can't save you, I'm afraid. You've lost too much blood. They're saying that had you been in the hospital when you did this, you might well have had a chance. Can you tell me why you wanted to do this to yourself?"

"That other man did it. He said he was going to kill me, and he did." It was costing him too much to talk, so he closed his eyes. Right there behind his closed lids, the man was standing there.

"They won't believe you when you tell them I killed you, Talbot. Trust me on that. I killed you because you're a horrible person, and you didn't deserve to live. Some people will think it wasn't my job to do so, but I wanted my daughters and son to sleep well at night, knowing that you're not out there lurking around to get them. I'm going to raise them to be fine upstanding people. Thankfully without you around. Good bye, Talbot."

William could no longer open his eyes even if he wanted to. His legs no longer worked either, and he was feeling light like he could float on air. Just as he was thinking that he was feeling better, William felt dead. Just like that, he felt like he'd died, and his last thought was he'd been treated unfairly by someone, and they were going to pay.

~*~

Cal hadn't told anyone about his part in the death of Talbot. He wouldn't have done it at all if Hammy hadn't given him permission. It was a fear of both of them that the idiot would get out on a technicality and be able to roam around hurting people as he had before. There were too many variables that could go wrong for them to just let the court systems do their duty for his children.

He thought perhaps Rosie had figured it out. She had asked him, point blank, if he'd been around when Talbot had died. Nearly telling her he had, he only shook his head at her, and she nodded. Then something that he hadn't expected from her, she hugged him tightly and thanked him. Since then, three days now, she'd not mentioned it to him or anyone else that he knew of.

Ruby was working at the clinic today with him. There was a family that needed some help that had come in, and he was working with the adults while Ruby worked with the little boy. Well, he was sixteen, but to him, he was nothing more than a baby. The parents were sort of closed-mouthed on saying much about why they were there. He was nearly ready to ask them if they wanted to have another appointment, thinking it was just too close to the man's mother's death to be seeing someone when the wife spoke up.

"The doctor that's talking to Jimmy, is it a female?" An odd question, but he did answer her. "I'd rather he didn't see a woman doctor. Jimmy doesn't do well around women. You should go and find out if she's having any headway with him. Just to be sure."

Under normal circumstances, he would have told the couple that his partner was capable of handling anything, that she was a good doctor, but a finger of fear ran up his spine, and he stood up. The man did as well, following him out the door to where Ruby was working. The door was open, and he found that he didn't want to enter the room without back up. Just as he was going to call Hammy to come to him, Robin came down the hall.

Warren was right behind her.

"Something wrong?" He nodded and then told Warren that he wasn't sure. "All right. Robin, honey, stay here with this gentleman, please and Cal and I will check things out."

Just like that, Warren believed him and Robin, his mate, were going to help. The closer they got to the open door, the more terrified he became. Warren called out to Ruby, and when they didn't get an answer, they both rushed to the room.

Blood was everywhere. He saw Ruby lying on the couch, but she was sitting up, talking to Warren when he asked her if she was all right. When a smart slap to his face brought him back to the present, not sure where his head had been, Warren told him to call the police. Nodding, not looking around, he left the room and had their secretary to call the police. Then he reached out to Hammy.

"Come to the Clinic. Now." He appeared in the room in a matter of seconds. Hammy sat him down on the chair that his secretary had been in and had him put his head between his knees. Robin was speaking to someone he could only assume that it was the boy's father.

The mother was still in his office, but she was

screaming. Finally having enough, he turned to her and told her to shut the fuck up. Her mouth snapped shut like he'd hoped it would. If he were to have been asked what their names were at that moment, he was positive that he'd not be able to tell anyone. It wasn't until Ruby came out of the office that he started to sob. She was covered in cuts and bruises and blood all over her clothing.

After being warned four times not to touch anything. He finally realized that she was covered in evidence. The police were there. Cal had no idea how long they'd been there. He let himself focus on one thing, and that was Ruby. So long as she was up and moving around, he knew she was alive. But his mind and his heart were having trouble with everything else that was going on in the area.

"Dr. Meyers?" He looked at the officer. "Can you listen to me? I need to ask you a few questions, all right?"

It took him a few minutes to realize that the officer wasn't talking to him but Ruby. His grip on his emotions were getting the better of him, and it wasn't until Warren put his hand on his shoulder quite hard that he was better able to handle himself.

"Branchlet." The officer turned to him. "I'm sorry. That's their names. Robert and Malison Branchlet. Their

son is Bob. I'm sorry. I couldn't remember, and it just…
I'll be quiet now."

Robert sat down next to him with strict orders not
to talk. Cal didn't want to hear whatever he was to say,
but he did reach out beyond the room into Ruby's office.
He was looking for Bob. The sixteen year old boy. There
wasn't any heartbeat or anything coming from him. Cal
made his way to his wife. He needed to know if she was
all right.

*"I'm all right. When I get out of here, I'm going to hug
the fuck out of whoever gave me immortality. I would be dead
if not for that. Oh, Cal, I'm truly all right."* He let out a long
breath so hard that he hurt from it. *"I'm all right, Cal. I
promise you. Bob killed his grandmother when she wouldn't
allow him to go out. She'd caught him sneaking out of the
house, and he murdered her. Then he came up with this story
about how someone had come into the house and killed her and
robbed her. When I asked him how he'd managed to survive, he
came at me with a switchblade and stabbed me several times.
There wasn't any time for me to react. All I did was hold out
my hand to keep him away, and he flew across the room hard
enough to slam into the wall and break his back. That didn't
stop him, either. I have magic. Magic enough to keep him away
from me long enough for me to be able to kill the little fucker. I*

would have called to you, but for the life of me, I simply forgot. I was so focused on keeping alive than I was calling for help. It went down that fast. Cal, I think the parents knew he'd done it too."

"I love you, Ruby. So much, honey." He saw Rosie come into the room and stood up to stop her from messing with evidence. *"Talk to your sister, Ruby, or she's going to kill someone to get to you."*

Cal saw the moment that Ruby spoke to Rosie. She went limp in his arms, and he held her close to him as she sobbed. Then when she started asking him if he was all right, she nearly knocked him out of the chair, checking out his poor body. To have them both, all right, was more than he could have hoped for in all his life. Christ, he might even hug Hammy a bunch, too, for giving him immortality a long time ago and some of it to his wife and sister.

The police questioned everyone several times. He wanted them to finish up soon so that he could hold onto Ruby. However, they sent her to the hospital to have some of the smaller wounds looked at. He told them that he'd not entered the room for a moment and hadn't touched anything so he could stay at the office.

The parents of Bob were both arrested for

harboring a fugitive. Not only did they know that he'd killed his grandmother, but they'd hidden the knife that he'd used as well as cleaned up the blood around the house. That was when it came out that Bob had also killed two babysitters when he'd been younger and hadn't mentioned that when they came to see him and Ruby. They were going to be in jail for a very long time, he hoped.

Bob was dead. The police said that the reason Ruby was able to toss him across the room like she had was because she'd been afraid. Adrenaline had given her what she needed to get him away from her, and that was all that was said about it. Not only was Ruby not going to be charged, but she was considered a hero by most of the people in the town. Cal thought it would be a long time before either of them took on a patient without a full background check of not just their lives but their mind as well. No more surprises like this again.

When she was released from the hospital, she was wearing a pair of scrubs that were slightly too big for her and a towel around her head. Hugging her now that he could, Cal found he didn't want to let go of her. Ever. Just holding her made him feel like she was all right, but he couldn't let go of her. It wasn't until Rosie shoved him out of the way that he remembered that he had to share her. It was hard, but he was actually afraid that Rosie might well hurt him if he didn't share.

Rosie picked up some food for them to have for dinner while he took Ruby home so that she could shower again and put on her own clothing. Joey was there with Missy, and they both seemed excited to see them. After explaining what had happened, having decided earlier in their new family that they'd not lie to her, they settled down in the living room to eat pizzas and drink soda while enjoying a funny movie. The four of them also traded around holding the babies, which he had to admit made him feel a good deal better about life.

It was around midnight when they all went to bed. Rosie was going to spend the night with them, she needed to be close to her sister, and Missy slept in the babies' room so that she could be nearer to them. He was glad now that they'd put in an extra bed in the babies' room so she could do that when she wanted.

Once Ruby was sleeping, he got up and went out into the yard. He needed a good long run as his other half and was just getting ready to shift when he heard a noise in the back of the yard. Calling out to ask whomever it was to show themselves, he was surprised to see that it was Marshall Morton. A wolf shifter that he'd met and had become friends with a long time ago.

After hugging each other, he could tell the other man wasn't well. He was not sick, but he was fighting some kind of demons that were haunting him. Sitting on the deck with him, he asked him if there was anything that he could do for him. Anything.

"I'm not sure what I need at the moment. I only came by to talk to Hammy for a bit, but I found that he has his own mate. You as well, I see." He told him about Ruby and her sister. Then he went on to explain how he'd also inherited a family with a teenager as well as twin infants. "Only you would take on a family so early in your relationship with your new mate. I can't wait to meet this woman. She'd have to be something special in order to stick with you."

"You'd be surprised how many times a day I think that very same thing. How are you, Marshall? Is there anything that I can do for you?" He said that he had to do some traveling soon, but he'd be back. "Is it about your family again?"

"It is, as a matter of fact. My father, mostly. He's being accused of not being an alpha, and someone wants him dead. I can't see my dad taking a position he wasn't suited for. And mom is beside herself with the things that are being said about dad. Do you suppose there will ever be a time when there isn't any strife in the world, and we can all just get along?"

"No. While it might be fun for a while, I see it as being fairly boring, don't you?" They both laughed. "How are your parents? I've not seen them in a very long time. Are they still the most romantic couple ever?"

"More so, I think. They're living for the day that I find my own mate and bring them lots of grandchildren. I don't think that there is anyone out there for me. I mean, Christ, I'm about as old as dirt now. Not to mention set in my ways. What sort of woman would want to hang her hat with me when I'm old enough to have been around when the world was nothing more than fields of trees and wild animals."

"You'd be surprised. Did you know that Hammy is the king of vampires? And Lander, his wife, my goodness, Marshall, she was born to the job. She is compassionate as well as a hard ass. I love her to pieces. But I'd never cross her. Robin, Warren's mate, is wonderful. She's witty as well as smart. Ruby is a child psychologist."

"I heard about what happened today. It's what brought me here to see you. Is there anything I can do to help out?" He said that the police were handling it for now. "I bet that's going about as fast as molasses on a cold day. I'll keep my ear to the ground while I'm fixing things up for my parents. If you need anything, just let me know."

"You're leaving? Already?" He said that he had a lot of things on the burner and needed to put out a few flames too. But that he'd be back soon. "I hope so. I miss you, old man."

When Marshall moved toward the wooded area that he'd come from, Cal sat there for a long while watching the sun come up. It was the first time in some time that he'd felt like he was on the right track. Of what? He didn't have a clue, but he was feeling good about things.

Getting up, he made his way into the house to start on breakfast. Missy joined him first, bringing the babies in one at a time and putting them in their bassinet. Once they were settled, she helped him with breakfast. It wasn't long before the rest of the family joined them. Cal thought it was a perfect start to a day. And he couldn't have been happier about having a family around him.

Chapter 6

"What the fuck is the matter with you?" Missy looked at Ruby and then Rosie when she asked her what was wrong. "You've been snapping and nipping at people for the last two days, and I'm frankly sick of it. If you have something to say, then fucking say it. All this picking fights with me is getting on my last nerve."

"You killed my sister. You let her die when there was no reason for it." The moment the words were out of her mouth, Missy knew that she'd pissed off both women. "She didn't have to die. No one dies in childbirth anymore. Why?"

No one said anything for a full ten minutes. Ruby

kept staring at Rosie, and Rosie just stared at her. She was glad now that Cal had left on a business trip with his grandda. There was no telling what he might have said to her. Missy was so pissed off right now she had a feeling that her head was going to explode in the pain that she'd been carrying around since the death certificate had been mailed to her three days ago.

"Nothing to say? You don't even want to tell me you're sorry?" Rosie told her to come with her. "I'm not going anywhere with you. Get out of my life. I want nothing to do with you."

Rosie walked toward her, and it was the first time in her life that she'd seen so much anger on someone. Heat billowed off her body the closer she got. And when she was standing only inches from her, she spoke to her quietly and hard.

"I'm not going to tell you again to get into the fucking truck." When she turned on her heel and left the kitchen, it was Ruby that spoke this time.

"You'd better go with her, Missy. She won't hurt you, but you have to learn a few things, and I, for one, am glad that you're going to get the truth." She asked her about what. "Your sister."

When the truck started up, she made her way out

of the house. If she was honest with herself, Missy was terrified of Rosie. The few things that she'd read about her when she'd done a search about her made her realize that Rosie wasn't just in the special forces, but she was the head of it. She also had been honored by the President several times over her career. Not that Missy was ever going to believe or like her, not ever, but she knew that she was one scary fucking bitch.

When the truck stopped, it took her a few moments to realize they were at the clinic where Bethy died. Every time she passed this way when riding with someone, it would bring tears to her eyes. Not once had she been able to see her sister after her death. The casket had been a closed one, per Bethy's wishes, and it had only been a graveside service. Her wishes had been handwritten and witnessed by a doctor in the clinic the night before she died. Before, she was murdered by Rosie. When Rosie didn't get out of the truck, neither did she.

"Do you want the truth, or do you want to go on believing whatever story you concocted in your head as being the truth?" She told her she knew what had happened. "You think you do, Missy. But you aren't even close to knowing shit. I do. I was there for the last part of it, but I also was the one that performed the autopsy on her after her body was delivered of the babies. The state coroner was on duty with me, but as he'd broken his arm in a skiing accident, he stood over me while I did the actual autopsy." She looked at her again. "The truth or not."

"Truth. But if you tell me you didn't murder my sister, I won't believe you." Without saying a word, Rosie got out of the truck and made her way to the front entrance. As they entered, they made a left to the elevators she'd never noticed before. Rosie had to badge into them in order for the doors to open. Three floors down, the doors opened again with another swipe of her badge, and the wall across from them professed that they were entering the morgue.

Rosie got off and turned to her right. Missy wasn't sure that this was a place she needed to be, but she followed. It would be just like her to leave her down here to be found by somebody bringing in a body. When they entered the large lab-like-looking room, Rosie used her keys to open a door that led to a beautifully appointed office. On the door was Rose Thimble, MD, State Coroner, then beneath it were the words Federal Bureau of Investigation Medical Examiner.

Telling her to have a seat, Rosie handed her a thick

file. She could see that there were pictures in it. Lots of paperwork too. On the top was her sister's name, along with her date of birth and death. She asked her why she thought that she wanted to see this.

"It will tell you exactly what happened the day that your sister died. She committed suicide." Shaking her head, Rosie nodded. "She was gone by the time I was called in to deliver the babies. If I had not been called, they wouldn't have been able to save Nathan, Liz either, for that matter. She was born second."

"You're lying." Rosie told her she would never lie to her about a thing like that. "She had no reason to kill herself. She wouldn't have done that without speaking to me about it."

"Would you have tried to talk her out of it?" She told Rosie that she would have been able to. "Then perhaps that's the reason that she didn't tell you. She did leave a note, but it wasn't addressed to you. I wanted you to read it that night, but my sister, already in love with you as her daughter, said it would be too much for you."

She opened the file and then closed it quickly. Taking in a deep breath, she tried again. This time she could see some of the photos, all of them in color, slipping around in the file. That was when Rosie began talking.

"Beth had it planned out to the moment. She was taking no chances that she could live beyond the birth of the children. In her note, she explained that had she been given the opportunity to abort them, she would have the day she found out she was pregnant. As it stood back then, it was difficult for her to run with you, keeping you safe and outwit your parents. When the two of you were finally settled, it was far too late to go to a doctor." Missy asked if she had said why she didn't want to have the babies. "When she was first pregnant, neither of you had any idea that it was twins. She knew that it was going to be a burden on the two of you, and her second plan was to leave it at a fire station. But even that was difficult for her to arrange. There was no way, she said in the letter, that you'd allow it. And for as much as she loved you, she despised the baby. Mostly, she said, the way she was impregnated. Did she ever tell you that the child was your alleged father's, William Talbot?"

"No. No, it couldn't have been. That man, Perkins, he said that they were his. Wait, alleged father?" Rosie when on to explain that she and Beth weren't sisters. The people that raised them had kidnapped them when they were still infants. "That can't be right. They said we were sisters. How do you know this? You're lying again."

"I told you that I'd never lie to you, Missy. And I'm not. Both your and Beth's biological parents were killed, and there wasn't any way to find you when you were taken. It was thought that you had both been killed the night your parents had been, and your bodies had been buried someplace. You and Beth, you're not blood-related to each other, nor to the people that raised you." Little things started to sink into her brain. Things that Beth said to her that now were coming to light. "The reason that I was able to find out is that when your sister's blood was put into the database after we figured out that she wasn't blood-related to either Janet or William, we found a match to a couple who had had their child taken when they were killed in Kentucky. Beth's last name was Hemmingway. Your last name is Jackson, and you were born in Wyoming. After a blood test from you, it was found that none of you were related. However, the twins do match William Talbot."

"Beth knew it. She mentioned it in the letter that she wrote." Rosie nodded. "Why didn't she tell me? I think that is something that I deserved to know. Don't you?"

"You're being told now, and you don't believe

me. Why would anyone think you would have believed anything she told you back then?" There was that. When she didn't want to hear things that upset her, Missy wouldn't believe it. "I don't know when or how Beth found out the truth. She left a key to a safety deposit box for Ruby to use to get all the paperwork that she'd found while living with the Talbots. Beth didn't want to have the babies. Nor did she want to live after they were born. She was terrified that, at some point, she'd end up killing them and you if she didn't remove herself from your lives. Once my sister and Cal decided they'd raise you, she knew she'd be able to take care of you and the babies and not have to hang around her words anymore. Beth hated herself and her thoughts about killing the three of you."

"Where is the letter now?" Rosie told her that it was in the file. "You kept it for me. You...no, Ruby wanted to destroy it, and you kept it for me so that I would someday know the truth."

"I wanted you to know the truth from the beginning. My sister thought it would be too hard on you to know that the girl that you loved had such thoughts in her head. Ruby asked me to be the one to tell you. Because she knew that it would come up someday, and she didn't want you to hate her when you found out what had happened."

"You said that she killed herself. That Beth was dead when you arrived at the clinic. How?" Rosie told her that it was horrific. Did she really want to know? "Yes. No. But I think I have to know. I need to know at what lengths she went to so that she could end her life."

"All right. Beth wasn't able to get out of bed during the last few weeks of her pregnancy. She was having troubles, you see. High blood pressure. Swelling all over her body. So she needed to — Missy, I'm going to be totally honest here. Beth could only use a bedpan when she needed to use the bathroom. That evening, after she said she was going to go to sleep, Beth put her arm in the bedpan that had been left in her room and used a fork to stab her wrist ten to fifteen times with it to cut her wrist. When I was called in to deliver the babies, no one had any idea she'd done that. It wasn't until they started to move her to the operating room that the pan hit the floor and dumped the blood everywhere. By then, she was already gone. She had died about a minute before I arrived."

"And the babies? Were they all right?" She told her that Cal had saved Nathan so that he'd be able to live, and she arrived in time to save Liz. "They were dead as well, then. My sister's plan was to kill them both and herself."

"We believe so. That's why she didn't call out to anyone when the labor began after her body began to shut down." Missy opened the folder again, this time looking at the pictures. There were a great many of them too. The wrist where she'd cut herself. The mess that was made of her arm when she was stabbing herself. There were even marks on her belly too from the fork that made her realize that Beth wasn't the person that she thought she was. To her, Beth was a monster.

"Is there more? I'm sure that there is. What else happened that day?" Rosie's phone rang about then, and she apologized that she had to take it. All Missy could think about was all the things that she'd said to this woman, and she was telling her sorry for taking a phone call. As soon as she hung up, Rosie said that she had someone coming in. That she'd make arrangements for someone to come— "No. Please. I'll stay in this office, but I need to have some quiet time right now. To think about—I'm not a nice person, am I? I've been so cruel to you and the others, but especially to you. I don't think there are words that I could say what would show how very sorry I am about—"

"Missy, no matter what bloodwork has come from this, you're still my niece. My sister and Cal still want you as their daughter and that of your niece and nephew. You've been dealt a shitty hand of no making of your own. I will say that I believe Beth had mental issues. She needed help, and it wasn't there for her. On top of being raped repeatedly, both of you your entire lives, she was dealing with a pregnancy at only fourteen years old and fifteen when she gave birth. I believe she took that course of action because she didn't know how to deal with it. She wasn't able to get help without fear of someone catching up to the two of you. What she did, yes, it was terrible, but to her way of thinking, it was the only way that she could deal with it. The only way that she could make her children and even you safe from all the monsters that were in your lives."

While Rosie went to work on the body when it came in, Missy looked at every page in the file. She read the letter that she had written and could see that Rosie was correct. Her sister, that was the only way that she would ever think of her, did what she thought was right for all concerned. Her heart broke, not just for Bethy but for her babies too.

~*~

Ruby was afraid when Rosie and Missy didn't come home by six. It was nearing seven when they both came in the door, and they were laughing. Ruby had to hold onto a chair to keep from falling down when she realized things must have gone better than she'd hoped. As soon as Missy saw her, Rosie said she was going home to shower. She hugged her so tightly that she wasn't sure that she ever wanted her to let her go.

"I'm so sorry. You…I shouldn't have treated any of you the way that I have been. Rosie let me read over my sister's file, and I understand a lot of things that I didn't before. But the worst part was that she felt like she had no one to turn to. Not even me." Ruby let the tears fall as she listened to Missy. "I'm not allowed to say that I'm a terrible person, Rosie said she'd find out, but that's what I feel like I have been. Rosie…Aunt Rosie said that I'm allowed one mistake, and while this isn't that one, she's going to make sure that I have help when I need it and that I know, daily and hourly, that I'm loved. I love you so much, Mom. If that's all right that I call you that."

"Yes, of course, it is. Oh, Missy. I have to admit that I was afraid that Rosie was going to be too hard on you, but now that I see you like this, I'm very glad that she was. She's a strong person, and I think we can all learn from her on this." Missy said that she'd learned not to piss her off. "Yes, well, I've known that since we were children. She's very vocal when she has a point to make. Listen, Cal isn't going to be home until late. He has something to do with the bruin that he's with. I had no idea that was what you called the group of bears. I'm going to have to get myself a list of things so that I'm at least able to keep up with things when he's talking to me. Why don't you and I have a nice dinner out and have some girly fun?"

Ruby loved having fun with Missy. She knew that she was going to have to be more disciplined toward her soon. Not only had Rosie pointed it out to her but Cal mentioned that he thought she was giving in to her too much. They were both right. She was going to have to be her mother as well as her friend. So when school was brought up, she did firmly put her foot down about her being able to drop out of school for a little while and picking it up later.

"No. You have to go to school. Not only that but if you're thinking of not going to college, that isn't going to be an option either. You have an opportunity to go to any college you wish anywhere. There is money for you to use so that you won't have to work that much while there. But you won't be able to get anywhere in this world if you don't have a good education." She told her that she didn't even know what she wanted to be. "You have plenty of time to figure that out between now and when you're ready to go. If that's your plan, then you're going to have to tell Cal and Rosie your plans."

"That's a good threat." They both laughed. "All right. I'll start looking into things. I was fascinated with the things that, by doing an autopsy on Beth, how much information there was to be found. I wonder because she's so brilliant, if any other doctor would have been able to find out the information that Rosie did."

"I'd like to say that my sister is as brilliant as there is, but she's not. However, she does do such a thorough job that she finds things about or on bodies quickly. I know that it's nothing that she came up with, but our parents said it to us all the time. If a job is worth doing, it's worth doing right. She and I both have always believed in—once in college, Rosie got a B in one of her classes. You know what she did? She took the class again to get an A. I swear to you, Missy, she's a perfectionist. I love her to pieces, but she can drive a person insane at times."

"I love her. She's hard to get used to, I'll admit that, but I do love her. You and Cal as well. The rest of the group? I'm still trying to get to know them. Hammy, he scares me to death. So does Lander but in a very different way. Like you know that she's smiling at you, but you don't know if she's simply smiling to get you off guard or she likes you." She told her that she felt the same way. "And her being a Queen Vampire? Well, I don't think there is a person in the world that is more scary than that."

They talked about this and that. Mostly to do with the twins. They were not calling them the babies anymore but calling them by their given names more often than not. Which she loved. Liz looked just like her mother had. The blond hair and all. But Nathan must have looked like his father. His hair was light brown but with streaks of gold in it. He had, even for as young as he was, a handsome face.

"I do have some things that I need to talk to you and Dad about. By the way, I called you mom earlier, and you didn't say anything, so I'm going to keep it up. Neither Beth nor I either one called them Mom and Dad, so I'm good with calling you guys that. You're much nicer than they ever were, anyway. Never mind. I know I'm only fourteen, and I'll be fifteen in November, but I want to talk about getting a part-time job because I can, not because I need food. I'd like to buy myself a car on my own and then go to college. I always wanted to go, but yanking your chain is so much fun. I don't know what I want to be or what I want to study, but I do want a job of some sort. Also, I don't want to tell Dad this, but I don't want to date. Not for a very long time, if ever. I know that I might grow out of it someday, but for now, I'm going to tell anyone who asks that I'm not permitted to date, and that should be the end of it once they see Dad. I just…I don't think that I can handle something like that. Do you know what I mean?"

"I do. While I've never had anything like what you went through happen to me, I can think that you'd have a hard time trusting any man. That brings up something that Hammy's grandfather brought up. He thinks that you need to see someone that you can talk to. Other than family. I know that sometimes I just need to vent, and it's easier to talk to someone I don't have a personal connection with. Grandda said not to go to either Cal or me in that either. Someone that you can just let loose with." Missy said that was her next thing. "Good. I'm so glad to hear that. Sometimes people think that they're all right with not having to talk to someone about what's happened to them but in the end, it really messes with their minds. It can take all kinds of forms of mental health when you just allow it to fester in your head and heart, so if you have anything, and I mean just anything, you ask one of us until we get someone that we trust to—"

"A woman." Ruby nodded. She could well understand that too. "Just because I think a woman might understand me more than a man will. I don't want…a man I'm not familiar with too might make me feel that I can't trust him."

"That can be arranged. I'll get on that as soon as tomorrow." When she heard from Cal telling them that he was home now, he decided to join them in town. They had to make a trip to the car to take some of their purchases out of the way. Not that they had spent too much, she kept telling herself, but she didn't want Cal to be crowded when he sat with them. She was glad that they'd done it when she saw that Grandda and Connie, Hammy's sister were with them.

"Next time you guys go, and you don't mind, invite me, please? I get a little starved for female company. We could even invite Robin and Lander. I'm sure that they'd love to have a girls' night out as well." Missy was all for it, but then she wasn't as used to the women as she was. They could be very blunt when talking about some subjects. Laughing to herself, she wondered what sort of input Missy could put into one of their conversations too.

Cal, as she knew he would be, was very good-natured about what they'd purchased. She'd not gotten much for herself, but Missy had an entire wardrobe now that she had desperately needed. They also picked up a few outfits for Nathan and Liz.

There were so many cute and handsome outfits for boys, Ruby thought, but not so many fall clothing for little girls. Liz was so tiny, being a twin, that it was hard to find her things to wear, like tights and long pants. Nathan, being just a little bigger, was able to wear newborn things easily. She knew that Liz would catch up soon. But Ruby was just a little impatient right now.

On the way home, she asked Cal about the meeting that he'd had with the bruin. He said that he didn't want to talk about it just yet but would when they were alone. Not one minute after he said that to her, he told her what was going on through their link.

"I'm to be the King of all Bruins. They have been watching me for decades, apparently and knew that when the current king was ready to step down, they were going to figure out a way to talk me into doing the job. I told them I needed some time to think about it. I have a month." She asked him why he would turn it down. "Mostly to do with you."

"Me? I'm not even a bear. Why would it have to do with me? You'd be king, not me." He told her. "No, I can't be the queen of bears. I'm sorry, Cal, but I'm—I think I might have mentioned this to you before. I'm not a bear. I'm just plain old Ruby, mother to three children."

"Yes, you're my mate too. And our children would be princes and princesses too. Next in line to able to take over for me if you and I wished to step down or take some time off. Missy would be the one that would run things in our absence." If he said anything else to her about anything, even that he was going to have a baby or something. She hadn't heard. It wasn't until they were stopped in front of their home and he was asking her if she was going to get out that she looked at him. "Are you all right?"

"I have no idea." She pulled out a few of the bags only to have him take them from her so that he could carry them. "Are you being macho right now so that I don't hurt you?"

"Yes. And yes." He laughed when she glared at him. "I'm afraid of you when you have that look on your face. It's all cute and innocent, but I know that in a moment's notice, you can turn on me like a bear." He kissed her as he walked by her.

She took the last two bags out of the back of the car. One held two pairs of infant shoes. The other held some warm socks that she was going to wear all winter to keep her feet warm. She wondered if she should put them on to beat the snot out of Cal for springing things onto her and being adorably wonderful to her at the same time. When she got to the kitchen, the place they ended up most of the time when they were home, Missy was telling him about the things she was planning about a part-time job.

Making her way up to the nursery, she let them talk. They both needed to be her parents, and neither of them had to be there when they were talking. Right now, she needed some cuddle time, and Nathan was wide awake and seemingly waiting for her to come to get him. Liz was snoozing.

"How is mommy's little boy today? Have you been good for Jane?" Nathan was only three weeks old now, but it had to her seemed as if he'd been a part of her life forever. "You and your sister are going to be such heartbreakers when you get old enough."

She rocked him a little more, and he continued to

watch her face. So she told him what his daddy had said to her before getting out of the car. Tisking at Cal for his timing, she told Nathan that she wasn't going to be the kind of queen that everyone might expect. She was going to be a good but firm leader.

"Like you are as a mother?" She turned and looked at Cal when he spoke. "You're going to be perfect. You give me the word, honey, and I'll tell them whether or not we're going to be taking the job. The great part of it is we don't have to move. With the invent of being able to talk over phones and computers, we can hold all meetings that way. Also, we get all kinds of perks too."

"What sort of perks? Do you mean a crown? No thanks. Even wearing a hat does nutting things to my hair. What is it you think you can entice me with?" He named a few. "A jet. Whatever for? We'll go commercial so that we don't pollute up the air any more than we have to. As for having vacation homes all over the world? I don't know about that. Vacations for me have never happened, so we'll have to test the waters on that one. What else?"

"I get to fuck the Queen of all bears." It embarrassed her that he said that in front of Nathan, and when she scolded Cal for doing it, he laughed and told her that he had no idea what that meant. "Besides, I'm going to be getting rid of everyone in the house, then I'm going to come up here and fuck your — sorry, screw your brains out."

She was still laughing when he took Nathan from her to change his diaper. As he was doing that, she went ahead and successfully changed Liz's diaper as well without waking the little girl. Tomorrow she was going to dress them in their new outfits. Ruby hoped Liz had enough hair to pull up into a little ponytail with bows that matched the little outfit that she'd picked out today.

Chapter 7

Murray didn't know what to think about the newly appointed town board members that were there as soon as he arrived at his parents' home. While they were standing around, talking to anyone that came by, and there were plenty of visitors at the home, he snuck his way into the large castle by pulling the shadows around him as he went to find his parents. He just happened to find his father first.

"Dad? What's with the news crews and police here? Has something happened?" Dad told him that it was a nightmare. "Dad, there are times when you think something is somewhat of a nightmare when it just takes a little adjustments here and there to fix. What's really going on?"

"The new board members, I'm sure you saw them, are saying they have decided to put a road through our land that will go right by the house with only mere inches to spare. And in that, they're going to have to tear down our home. I had no idea they were running a stupid road through—tell me, son, where would it go to or even, for that matter, come from? There is nothing beyond here but more of our land, and it just comes from the town that we mostly own as a starting point. They're not even going to—I'm not telling this well as I'm very upset. They only just sprung this on us this morn. And they're saying that the equipment will be here in the morning to tear it down. I've never—aren't they supposed to give notice of something like this? At least have a meeting with me? I'm in a fubble, son. A huge fubble."

"I'm not entirely sure what a fubble is, Dad, but let me see what is going on here." With the shadows drawn around him once again, Murray wandered around the yard and home to see what he could glean from other people's minds. Twice he heard that someone thought that the mayor was going to be living in the castle once it was updated, and then he heard that once the road was started, it would finish up right at the castle gates and be used as a tourist attraction when the road funding would suddenly disappear. Since there was very little money for anything like a single parking space, much less a road, he believed that one more. His parents were being dubbed.

Murray only knew one person who could get to the bottom of things, and that was his good friend, Brad Kirk. The man was like a dog with a bone. Chewing on every inch of it until he got all the marrow or, in this case, information that he could out of it before he was ready to say that he had all there was to have. And he would have it too. The man was a diligent investigator when someone asked for his help.

He'd been around for such a long time that Murray was surprised that he'd been buying up land not far from where his parents lived. Reaching out to him to see what he might be able to dig up, Kirk was just as happy to hear from him as he was contacting him.

"You're not going to believe this, but I read about this shit in this morning's paper. I even went back a few years looking online, and there isn't one mention of this road to nowhere going on. If what you're saying is, in fact, the truth of the matter, Hamish will need to be involved. Since he's king, no one can buy or sell land without giving him first dibs on it.

It's not his rule, but one that has been around for a long time. I mean, you can still inherit it from your father, but if you were wanting to sell, he gets to be the first to turn it down. I think it has something to do with the money owed to baby vamps that might turn up later to claim the land or something like that." Murray said that he remembered that law from a long time ago. *"I only just remembered it when I was looking into the land ownership. Also, the mayor nor the board members can simply buy up land that has been in a family for centuries by Eminent Domain by claiming that it's reasonably shown that the property is to be used for public purposes only. Also, they'd have to compensate them for all the land and the castle at fair market value. I don't think there is enough money in the entire town to show that they can do that, even with a loan from the state or country. I don't know how they'd be able to get someone to come in and value the land and the castle, but I would imagine that it would be in the hundreds of billions of dollars just for the castle and the lands around it. Doesn't that sucker sit on about fifty thousand acres?"*

He told him that his parents also owned more than half the land that the town was residing on, and they paid rent to his family to use the land for their government buildings as well as roads and homes.

"The rents, which aren't extraordinarily high from the

city for their rent they pay, has been behind for the last four or five years too." He thought of something. *"Could that be the reason this is going on? Do they want to get out of paying the rent they're being sued for? I know that the last time I was home, Dad had a law firm looking into just how to get the money from the cities."*

"I'll be there in a few days. Stall all you can. Call Hamish and let him know what is going on as well. He has the money and kingdom to toss around to get things going in the right direction." He told him about Cal and how he was now the king of all burin. *"Well, if that don't beat all. He should have been a long time ago if you were to ask me. All right, call him too. It might be funny to see a bunch of bears roaming around the land, scaring the shit out of people that have no right to anything that they're doing. This could be more fun than I thought it would be."*

Murray made sure to call Cal first. He knew that if he were to call Hamish first, he'd never get off the phone with him. He'd want every detail about his family, including his brother and sister, then he'd ask about his parents before he ever got to the point where he could tell him what was going on. Even then, he'd want details he wouldn't have until Brad got back to him. Cal was still laughing when he hung up with him, telling him that there was a fairly large burin right around there of about a thousand bears, and he'd have them roaming the property to keep it safe. Murray couldn't have asked for better news. Then he called Hamish.

After explaining to his wife as Hamish was taking care of some stupid shit—her words—with his new job, she'd help him out. She sounded like she was going to not just help him out, but also she was going to have the best fun ever in helping him. Yes, Murray thought, he was going to enjoy this much better.

About thirty minutes after talking to Lander, he got a call from someone by the name of Rosie Thimble. She asked if she could speak to the man in charge, however, if there was an FBI agent there, the highest ranking one. While he didn't know how to tell one from the other in the way of rank, he did find someone to help him with that.

He didn't walk away. It was his phone, after all. He could hear the woman's voice. She was screaming into the phone. The man listening on his end would say things like 'yes, sir' 'I'll get on that right now, sir' and other things that made him think that the woman on the other end had to be some ball buster to make a grown man sputter and spit like he was.

When the call ended and the phone was handed back to him, the agent walked away. Murray was positive if the man had had a tail, it would have been right between his legs. Since Murray didn't know if she'd hung up or not, he said hello into his cell phone. She asked him who he was.

"Murray Phelps. This is my parent's home that is being invaded by the idiots." She agreed with him that they were all fucking idiots. "Can I ask you what your part in this is?"

"Yes. I'm FBI. And since about twenty minutes ago, I've been promoted to Agent in charge of this shit storm. Like, I don't have a million other things that I should be working on rather than a land dispute with some moron that thinks just because his brother-in-law has a job working at the White House — as a dishwasher, I might add, that he could help his family take over homes of people that have been around a hell of a lot longer than the fucking White House where he works has been. Fucking stupid people. I hate them all." He couldn't help it. He laughed. She wasn't just honest as hell, but she didn't pull any punches when talking to people, either. "You'd not think this was so funny if you were where I am right now, trying to get an autopsy done by exhuming a body only to find out that there is no fucking body, not even sandbags, to make the weight of the thing believable."

"Are you coming here to this shit storm?" She told him that she didn't have much else to do, so she had to go there and roll some heads. "I'd like to see that. I'm betting all my fortune that you're going to do a very good job of it. What is going to happen anyway?"

"If that dumb fuck I just talked to does what I told him, the mayor, his wife, two children as well as the secretary, her staff as well as the Chief of police are going to be arrested. In addition to trying to accuse your father of being a vampire, which I do know that he is — defamation of character is a heavy fine when you're trying to take your family home because of racism." He asked her if her father was a vampire, then why would that be a reason to be called racism. "Sure, I don't care what your family is either, but the county seat can't write up a report about him being different, as in a vampire, in order to have him thrown off his land and his property — which they had no intentions of paying for, then that's against the law."

When she told him she had to go, he dejectedly hung up the phone. But he did mark her number in his caller ID with her name. In the event, he told himself that he had another question to ask her along the lines of asking her out to dinner or something.

The people that Rosie had mentioned had been arrested by the time he was in the yard again. Mom and Dad were sitting on the porch watching the events, too, when he sat down on the swing and joined them. A van pulled up about an hour later, and not only was it filled with more agents, but a woman dressed in jeans and a very skin-fitting blouse also got out too. The way she was talking, he just knew that this was the woman that had saved the day.

She didn't make her way up to the porch right away. Which he was fine with. Watching her ordering people around, once pulling out her gun and firing it into the ground, had him and his parents laughing. Apparently, the mayor thought of himself as well above a female FBI agent that carried a gun, and he was taken away in one of the city's new cruisers alone.

Hamish and his new mate also showed up. They didn't come up to the porch where they were before talking to two of the agents that had shown up with who he assumed was Rosie. She was pissed, every line of her beautiful body showed it, but once Hammy hugged her tightly in his arms, she seemed to calm down a bit. When she went back to the van, he thought for sure he was going to miss talking to her face-to-face when she reached in and pulled a large dog from the back.

The dog was hers. There was no doubt about it when he matched her step to step, never leaving her side without a lead on him. Joey, Murray heard her calling him, kept up with her but never stopped looking around for whatever might hurt his mistress. Finally, she made her way to the house where he and his parents were.

Hamish introduced her as Cal's sister-in-law. Then he told her about his family's long history of being here in this spot. She was polite, very much so, but he could tell that she didn't like being held up when there was work to be done, but she tolerated it well. When he watched her turn her head when his father went to kiss her, he laughed again.

"You were the little shit on the phone." He said that was him. "You know, you could have told me that it's your family that I was helping. I could have had you or one of them taking care of the mayor. Did you know that he's been stashing cash on the upper floors of the library that his wife has been using for her office? They've been crooks for some time now."

"I don't live here with my parents any longer, so, no, I had no idea what was going on until I came here to visit my family" He put out his hand to touch her in the guise of a handshake. "My name is Murray Phelps. I have a lot of titles, too, but that should help me learn your name."

The moment that he touched his hand to hers, he felt a feeling roll over him akin to his skin being set on fire. Not only his skin but where her fingers were touching his. He could feel the iciness of her anger like it was his own. Closing his eyes to the onslaught of not only her anger but every memory that she'd ever had. He could only wonder what she was getting from him.

~*~

Cal had no idea what had happened to Rosie or Murray, but every time he looked at him, he would burst out laughing. Not only was he still unconscious, but his forehead was bleeding still, and he was sure that the old vampire had broken a couple of fingers trying to hold onto Rosie when she was blasted away, much like Warren told him that he had when meeting Lander for the first time. When Murray sat up in bed, yelling out Rosie's name, he laid him back on the bed and told him to calm down.

"Where is she? She's powerful." Cal said that he'd gotten that too. "Where is she, Cal? I think she's my mate."

"According to her, and if I were you, I'd take this as gospel, she's not going to be anyone's plaything until she says so. Not to mention, being married or mated to a man that has no more sense than to get himself fixed up before being put to bed is going to expect her to baby and coddle him, and she'd rather stake you than to be around your whiney ass. What did you say to her when she helped you up off the floor?" He said he didn't remember that at all. "I'd start with that. It might, well, more than likely not go over better than you telling her you're her mate again. I think you've told her nearly a thousand times since the two of you were blasted apart."

Cal laughed again. "Now, what's so funny?" He laughed harder. "Tell me what you find so funny, or so help me. I'm going to kick your ass three weeks into next year."

"You. My god, Murray, how long has it been since we've been all together? Marshall isn't here yet, but he's on his way, and Hammy's grandda is having a grand time having all these beautiful women coming around all the time. He's just the same as he was all those years ago too." Murray asked again where Rosie was. "She's working. I'll tell you now that she's a great nurse but a better doctor than I've ever met. Right now, she's working on something for the hospital that has needed attention for some time. She and her sister they're also working at the Health Plex part-time until we can get it up and running better. It's doing well, but it needs some of the things that no one ever thinks about when they're putting together someplace for people to get help. Understand?"

"Yes. Can I go and see her, or will that just be causing me more pain?" Cal told him he hadn't any idea as he tried very hard to stay on her good side. "Probably a smart move. The only times I've spoken to her she seems to fly off the handle pretty easily."

"Usually, she doesn't. She's calm and cool. But when she's upset, there is no comparison to her anger. To say that she doesn't suffer fools easily is an understatement. When we hired a head of surgery for the clinic we're funding, he told her that she'd be better off being his secretary rather than an RN. He had no idea she was a better-qualified doctor than he was at being a man. I kid you not, Murray. She's got balls too. If I were her mate, I'd just step back and let her run the show. She's not much into cuddling, either. Just the opposite of

Ruby, her sister. Though here lately, she's just as bad. I love them both."

Getting out of the bed for Murray seemed to be a lot more difficult than he thought it should have been for the man. Deciding to take him to the hospital to see Rosie seemed like a better idea, even if it was to have her pissed off. Whatever had zapped him when they touched seemed to have had no effect on Rosie at all but had seemingly all but drained Murray all the way to his toes.

On the way to the hospital, he pointed out some of the projects they were working on. The new grounds for the schoolyard were the best, he thought. While driving around, they came across his daughter with the babies, and he introduced Murray to them as well. By the time they were at the hospital, Murray was dozing off and on and didn't look all that well. Almost as soon as they entered the hospital, Murray asked for a wheelchair and for his mate. Reaching out to Rosie, she came to him quickly.

Taking him to her office, Cal stayed with the couple. He was worried. More worried than he had been about anything else in his life. Once he was wheeled into the office, the door was locked and the shades drawn.

Hamish appeared in the office when Rosie simply stood in the middle of the room and shouted his name. One look at Murray, and he asked Rosie what she wanted to do.

"How the fuck am I to know what to do? You're in charge of shit. Fix him up so that he doesn't look like every horror picture show they've ever made about vampires. You're the ding dong in charge." Hamish glanced at him, then turned back to Rosie. Whatever she thought of, she wasn't the least bit happy about it. "Oh, you have got to be kidding me? He needs my blood? Mother fuck, I don't even want him, much less his munchers in my neck. That's what it is, isn't it? He's hungry, and I'm the only one who can feed him. Like I'm on the menu or some bull fucking shit as that."

"He's been hurt, or it might not be as —"

"I didn't hurt him, damn it. Whatever happened just happened. Why do I have to be the one that gets all eaten up because he wasn't smart enough to have a hardy meal before coming home to see his mom and dad?" Hamish said that if she didn't help him, he would die. "And if I say no, you're going to blame me for the rest of my life. Hell, even if you didn't, I would. All right, but no fucking around. I just want to feed him and send him on his way. I did point out to you earlier that I had a shit load of stuff to do today, and it's not going to be getting done while I'm hooked up to him like a shank of beef."

After explaining to her what needed to be done, she was no less pissed off about it. But she did make them promise not to leave them because she was afraid that he'd drain her dry. Which was a good argument. If he was this weak, then he was very hungry. With her being his mate and him nearly on death's doorstep, Murray might hurt Rosie without knowing it. Sitting on his lap facing him, Hamish opened a vein on her wrist for him to get a taste. Then when he was ready to feed, he'd help her by opening the larger one in her throat. Yeah, Cal thought, this could be very dangerous for Rosie.

Once Murray took a few sips from Rosie's wrist, he took her throat. He had to keep reminding himself that in normal times Murray wouldn't be this violent with his mate, but it took both him and Hamish to keep him from killing his mate. Once he had enough to heal himself, they asked Rosie to back away. They'd not realized how weak she was until she stumbled across the room and fell to the floor.

"We'll each give her a bit of our blood so that she'll be all right. He'll never forgive himself if he realizes what he's done to her." Cal said that he'd go first because of him not being a vampire and related to her. If that worked, Hamish wouldn't have to help Rosie out. Cal's blood was strong for being so old and King now, but she was still fading fast.

Hamish gave her a bit more than he thought he should have. But like Rosie had said, he would never forgive himself if he didn't help his friend's mate while she was down, especially after agreeing to help Murray.

It was several hours, and Hamish and himself giving both of them blood three more times. Whatever had happened, it wasn't anything either of them had encountered before. Murray woke up twice, asking for Rosie and between him and Hamish, they got the big man close enough to Rosie so that they could touch. Rosie never woke up in all this time.

"What's happening?" Cal and Hamish told Lander what had happened and what they had done to save their lives. "Do you think that you'll change her too? Like you did me?"

"Honestly, I've never thought of that. I only wanted her to get better." Hamish said he'd not be able to tell right away if she had, but he wasn't going to let it bother him if he did it. Or if she became a bear by all this.

"No, I think you're right. She's going to live, right? I'll even take any abuse she wants to hand out to me if she's around to do it."

The three of them watched over the couple for the next several days. They were able to take them to Hamish's home and put them in a room where the sunlight wouldn't bother them. They did find out that Rosie was now a vampire quite by accident because her skin burned badly when they were thinking of what room to put her in. In addition, they were able to get more help watching over them. Grandda didn't have any idea what had happened either, but whatever it was, they were getting better daily.

Ten days after they were blasted, it was Rosie that woke up first. She didn't seem to be terribly upset with finding herself in the big bed with Murray but did get up and go back to her house for a shower and a change of clothing or two. She also brought some toys for Joey to play with.

He'd never left her side while they were all watching over them but to go out and come back in after a bathroom break. Cal was worried about him because he wouldn't eat much but hoped that since he was in such good shape, it wouldn't harm him too much. He knew just how much the dog meant to Rosie, and she'd be terribly upset if anything were to ever happen to the guy.

After she returned with fresh clothing and her hair still damp, she asked what had happened. Cal knew better than to give her half-truths, so he told her straight up what had happened and what they knew. She took being a vampire all right, he thought, but she was concerned with Murray.

"Will he be all right?" Cal told her that he seemed to be getting stronger every hour since she woke up. "Is that a big deal? I mean, I know that I have some magic in me, thanks to you, but will it give him the willies when he finds out that I'm like him? A vampire?"

"I don't think he'll care overly much just knowing that you're alive. But it's been a very long time since I've seen Murray, so he might not be the same guy he was when we parted ways all those years ago. But I know if anyone can handle him, it would be you." She thanked him. "What else can I tell you? You've got some of my blood too. And as you knew, before this all started, I was bruin King, so I haven't any idea what my stronger blood would have done to you. Oh, your sister will be over later with the babies and Missy. She took them to get some dinner out because they were so worried about you. So had Joey."

Like he knew they were talking about him, the dog picked up his pink pig and held it in his mouth while looking at them both. When Rosie scratched him on the head, they both let go of a huge sigh of relief. It was normal to be petted again after so long, he supposed, but these two were so good together.

"I don't know what I'm supposed to do now." Cal told her that he wasn't sure what she meant. "I don't know, jackass. Do I have to be here with him all the time? Will he want another feast when he wakes up? I don't fucking know."

"You could ask me." They both turned to look at Murray when he spoke. "I don't think I've been up and around for a bit. Right now, I'm feeling like I've been run over. What the hell is going on?"

"You've been resting." Cal stood up before laughing. "I'll leave you with your mate. Oh, by the way, she's been changed into a vampire. Maybe even a little bit of bear. So tread carefully. I don't think she's fully aware of what went on with her body either."

Cal left them there after that. He was still laughing when he got home, where his own family was hanging out. After being given a fashion show with the things that were purchased, he went to the sublevels to take a long, much-needed nap. It had been just too hard on him the last couple of weeks.

Chapter 8

Ruby was enjoying the clinic. There were a lot of children that came into the place with their family members, and she would assess how they were handling having one or both of their parents getting dried out or even, most of the time, dying from their addiction. The older children, ten to fifteen, seemed to be the hardest for her to get through to. Most of the time, it was because they no longer believed the parent was ever going to stop whatever it was he or she was doing at the time to get them here. Jaded, she called them. They were much too young, in her estimation, to be so jaded about life like they were.

"Doc. Meyer's, your husband is on line two. He said that if you're too busy, he'll talk to you later." She said she'd take it. "I knew that you would. Like I said, he's on line two."

"I have some good news and some not so go news. Which do you want first?" Ruby asked him how not so good was the second news. "I have to go before the board, and you're supposed to go with me. Lander gave me some advice on that score and said that now that there is a king and queen, we don't need board members anymore. I think they might know that might happen to them since Lander had made a big deal about destroying them, and they want to talk about that."

She laughed. "I'm assuming that they want to make sure that they can just leave the job without having to die to do that. All right, if they're not too terribly stupid or have done too much wrong in the name of board members, they can go free. What's the better news? I'm hoping that it's as easy as the not-so-good news was." He told her that it was. "I found us a house. I know that we have one, but we're going to need a house where we can hold parties in gatherings when we have to host other people. I don't remember that ever happening since I've been around, but then I didn't know that we haven't had a king for about a thousand years either."

"So we need like a party house. But not necessarily a house." He said that was right. "Good, I like that idea of having a place like that. And if you'd not mind, we should build or have it built in the downtown area so that the town can use it if he needs to. A win-win for everyone, I believe. What else?"

He said that was all he had, and she told him what she was doing. "Why would you be working in the yard? I mean, when I left the house this morning, there were two inches of snow on the ground. What on earth are you doing that requires you to be out digging in the snow?"

"Peas. You can plant them in the late fall, and they'll have a head start on the first warm spell in the spring. I love fresh peas, and Nathan and Liz do as well. Missy isn't sure about them, but I told her that canned peas were terrible when compared to fresh right off the vine peas."

When he told her that he'd be home by five, she started gathering up the things that she wanted to take home to work on too. Missy was a great help in sorting things out for them both, and they were paying her to watch the twins when they needed a bit of extra time at home.

"I love them so much, don't you?" Ruby said that she didn't know love could be so instant when there was a baby involved. "Yeah, I know what you mean. When I went to pick up some paperwork for Aunt Rosie, I stopped by to see the new ones."

"There has been an unusual number of babies born over the last few months. I wonder what that is all about." She didn't want to talk about sex with her daughter, so she said it was good for the town to have fresh blood. "Or it could be that people like sex a great deal and are whooping it up, as Grandda told me."

"Grandda is going to end up with a bar of soap in his mouth if he doesn't learn to behave himself." The two of them laughed, and when Nathan was finished with his bottle, Missy gave Liz hers. "You do that so well, Missy. It's like you've been doing it all your life."

"It feels like it sometimes. Though not in a bad way." She had that serious look on her face before turning to look at her. "I know that they're not related to me at all, but I wonder if it would be all right if when they're told about their mom, we don't tell them that part."

Ruby didn't say anything, but she didn't agree with her at all about it. Before she could work up a plan to tell her what her opinion of it was. Missy was shaking her head before she began speaking.

"I don't think that would be the right thing to do either. Lying to them would make it so that they don't trust me. No, we have to tell them the truth." Ruby told her that it didn't have to be when they were so young. "Maybe, but then it's still a lie, don't you think? I mean, I did take Aunt Lander's advice and saved all the articles that I came across about the people who took us. The court hearing too. Even pictures of them that I could find when the police went to their house. They need to know. I know that I would have liked to have known some of the things going on while I was little."

After working it out on her own, telling Ruby that they'd be eating soon, her cell phone rang, and it was grandda. He wanted to have dinner with his favorite granddaughter. She was also his only granddaughter that had a cell phone, but that didn't matter. She went over to his house and was going to spend the night. Not long after Cal made it home, the nanny came to retrieve the younger children to bathe and put them to bed. It was only going to be her and Cal for dinner.

As soon as the house was quiet again, the two of them went into the living room. They were the only house that had a television in their living room. Also, as it turned out, it was the only television in their home. Neither of them bothered to turn it on but sat next to each other, talking about their day.

Turning when nothing more seemed to be important enough to talk about, Ruby turned and sat on Cal's lap, facing him. As she worked with the buttons to get them undone, she told him what her plans were going to be about what she was about to do to him.

"I think that this house is much too warm for you to be dressed up like you are. I mean, a bear wearing flannel? That makes no sense whatsoever." As soon as his shirt was unbuttoned, she began working it off his arms. "I think this would be easier if you were standing up, but then I'd not be able to feel your nice thick cock between my legs."

"Christ woman. You're nearly too much for me." He rolled her to her back and onto the floor. Once she was there, he stood over her and stripped off his pants and boxers at the same time. Tossing his shoes off when they tangled up in the pants, he grabbed her pants after she had undone them and ripped them to shreds getting them off her body. "You're mine."

It wasn't making love but a kind of animalistic kind of fucking. Everywhere he touched her, each time that he nipped at her skin, she would cry out about how wonderful it felt. She could feel her pussy dripping with her juices. And when Cal settled between her thighs, she screamed, loud and long, when she came hard.

His cock filled her over and over, and his mouth suckled at her breasts. Not just her nipples, which she loved, but her entire breast fit into his mouth. Cal moved up and down her body over and over, fucking her with his tongue and fingers, then his cock. Each time she came, powerful releases that nearly made her pass out, he would start again. She was so weak that she could barely beg him to stop long enough that she could catch her breath. When moved down to between her legs again, as if he were settling in for an all-night feast, she fainted dead away when he pinched her clit hard enough for her to see stars and loved every second of it.

When she opened her eyes, he was over her, his cock filling her slowly over and over while he suckled at her breasts. All she'd meant to do was to tease him a little, then head up to the bedroom. But he'd taken the lead right out of her hands and had given her the best sex of her life. Smiling up at her when he lifted his head, he told her he loved her.

"And I love you too." He fucked her harder

when she wrapped her legs around his waist. Never had sex meant all that much to her, but with Cal, it was everything. When he lifted her ass up from the carpet, pounding her just a little harder, she held onto him like her life depended on it. Once he moved his hips, his groin hitting her own, Ruby dug her nails into his back hard enough that she knew she'd drawn blood. Then everything went black.

When she woke up, she was in their bed. Looking around for Cal, she realized that her body was sore. Not just her muscles, but she was sure that she'd broken a couple of bones while they were at it. Cal saying her name had her turning to him, and when he moved to the edge of the bed, his body leaning over her, she kissed him when he offered her his mouth.

"You're going to have a baby." She just stared at him, thinking that he meant the babies they already had. "No. You were in heat. You might well have been before tonight, but we've both been so busy with getting the children settled that I didn't pay attention. My bear knew, of course, but I—"

"We have infants now, Cal." He told her that he was sorry. "Don't be sorry, but we're going to have three children under the age of one when this one is born.

You'd better be thinking of ways of being a very helpful daddy when they get here. Missy, she's wonderful, but I'm betting even she might run for the hills when we bring another baby home."

"You're not mad, are you?" She asked him what there was for her to be mad about. "What you just said, three babies under the age of one. I mean, I will be helpful, you don't have to worry about that, but I thought for sure that you'd want to strangle me. Lander had this saying she'd say to Hammy when he messed up that she was going to knock his fangs out and stab him to death with them. Everyone believes her too."

"Yeah, I would as well. She's a lovely person, but she scares the shit out of me. Missy loves her and doesn't seem to be too afraid of her. But me? I'm scared every time I see her that she's going to drain me or something." Sitting up, she had to lie back down. "I'm feeling weird, Cal. Is this what I can expect while I'm pregnant?"

"No. You're a bear." She nodded, then sat up again, this time holding her head while she glared at him. "Yeah, I didn't know that would happen either. We did have something about kings and queens about newly crowned burins would need a mate to their equal in an old tome that has been handed down from leader to leader. I got it out of storage when I woke up and knew you were changed. So if you had been a bear and not me, I would have been human. I guess. But since I'm a bear and as my mate, you weren't, now you are. I don't think I'm saying this quite right."

"So I'll be able to shift into a bear like you do." He said that is what the book said. "Cal, what do you think is going to happen when I go out into the yard and try to change into a bear? You'd better not be telling me that you don't know again. That's not so nice to dangle that kind of information in front of me only to take it away."

"You're right. But I don't know that there has been a burin king and queen for centuries. We're assuming, and that's all we can do at this point, that, like Lander, you were needed to be a bear queen, and she was a vampire queen. That's why it happened." She tossed off the covers and pulled his shirt over her body as she made her way out of the room. "We're doing this now? Honey, it's four in the morning. Don't you want to—"

"No, I do not want to wait. I can't believe that you'd even think that I would want to." She was still talking to him when she ended up in the front hall. "All that might happen is that my feet get too cold. I'll come back in here and sob because I'm not a bear."

She opened the door and nearly shut it again. The blast of arctic air nearly took her breath away. However, the more she moved around, the less sore she was, so that would be something to count on the win side if this didn't work.

"All you need to do is think of her. Sometimes you can see her there if you close your eyes. Do you see her?" She nodded. So overwhelmed by the sight of the beautiful bear looking back at her. "You can talk to her too. Ask her if she's ready or something."

"Hello, my lovely. My, but you are beautiful." She thanked her bear and asked her if she had a name to be called. "Most never name their other half, but I have a feeling that you and I will talk quite a bit. You may name me if you are wishing to, my lady. It would be a great honor to be named by one such as you."

"My mother's name was Lana. I should like to call you that in honor of her." Her bear bowed before her, and she did the same. "Shall we have a run, Lana? I'm so excited to be with you as a bear."

"My dear child, you are already." Looking down at her hands, she could see they were great paws. And they were the most beautiful shade of black she'd ever seen, like silk. "I wondered what color we would be. I have, over the centuries, been all colors of bruin. But you are my first queen. We shall go on forever, the two of us and have many cubs. Would you like to know the sex of your child?"

"Yes. I would." She told her what it would be and Ruby was so happy. "I should like to keep it a secrete for as long as I can if you'd not mind."

"No, that would be wonderful. I shant allow the king to even guess." She stood up on all four of her paws and tried to walk. "You are doing an amazing job, my lady. Run. No one would dare say a bad thing about you as you enjoy this new freedom with me."

~*~

It was nearing noon when both he and Ruby went into the house to rest. Lucky for them, he thought Missy was with grandda. What he'd been calling Hamish's grandda since he'd been a child knew that Ruby had been changed and that they were enjoying the day. When they got up from their nap, grandda told them to enjoy another night without their family as he and Missy were going to the movies. Something that he'd never thought that grandda had done before.

Getting dressed up to drive to Columbus, the two of them touched and kissed. It might well have been why it took them so long to get ready, but since they weren't on a schedule, they didn't care.

They talked about Murray and Rosie a great deal. As mates, they were going to have to temper themselves about their tempers. At least Rosie would. Then Ruby brought up about it would be wonderful if they were to have children right away so that they could grow up together.

Dinner was spectacular. They both enjoyed a steak dinner with trimmings, and then they had cheesecake for dessert. As it was still early, they decided to do a little shopping for the kids and wondered about Christmas decorations for the house. She'd never put up a tree after leaving home, and she told Cal that she didn't think Rosie had either. It was just the two of them most of the time, and they didn't want to bother.

"I've got a few things that I have to take care of once we're settled in as being king and queen. Lander mentioned how they got rid of their council once they figured out that they didn't need them anymore. They were crooks, I guess." Ruby said that Hamish had told her the same thing. "Also, Hamish had mentioned that we'd better be setting up times to meet with people, or they'd be coming around all the time. And he said to stick with it."

"Yes, I've actually started a list of things that he told me about too. I want to do this right, and using some of the things that happened to him when he first started is a good way for us to not make the same mistakes." The two of them talked about some other things that they'd been given advice on, and they were going to try and make as many things work out for them too. "Do you suppose that there hasn't been a king around for so long because they were waiting on you? I mean, I don't know that, but it seems like it's been a very long time, and there have been other strong bears born, don't you think?"

"I do. But I don't know. I've only just started on the books that I've found. Maybe you and I can read them and compare notes or something. Hopefully, they're all written in something that we can both read. The books from Hamish were written in Vampire, and Lander couldn't make it out before. But as soon as she was changed, she could read it."

"I never thought of that. I hope you're right." As they were making their way back home, full and so relaxed, they talked about the upcoming holidays. Cal told her that Hamish wanted to host Thanksgiving at their home because it would be his first in a very long time with friends and family around. Halloween is Warren's favorite holiday. He used to go all out when he was living in a large city. Maybe we can be our bears, and no one would ever know."

They were both laughing when they pulled into their drive. The house wasn't dark, with only just a few lights in some of the lower rooms. There was smoke curling from the chimney that she loved to watch against the stars. Ruby had to admit that she loved the colder weather and wondered if it had anything to do with her being a bear now.

There were two phone messages when they got in the house. One of them was saying that Missy was accepted in the high school they'd gone to when she needed to be tested for her grades. They wanted to advance her to the eleventh grade instead of the nineth, where she should have been. The second note was some Marshall Morton, the wolf friend of Hamish's, saying that he was going to be delayed a bit more, but he was coming to visit.

Before You Go...

HELP AN AUTHOR

write a review

THANK YOU!

Share your voice and help guide other readers to these wonderful books. Even if it's only a line or two, your reviews help readers discover the author's books so they can continue creating stories that you'll love. Log in to your favorite retailer and leave a review. Thank you.

AWARD WINNING, BESTSELLING AUTHOR

Kathi Barton, a winner of the Pinnacle Book Achievement Award and a best-selling author on Amazon and All Romance books, lives in Nashport, Ohio, with her husband, Paul. When not creating new worlds and romance, Kathi and her husband enjoy camping and going to auctions. She can also be seen at county fairs with her husband, an artist and potter.

Her muse, a cross between Jimmy Stewart and Hugh Jackman, brings her stories to life for her readers in a way that has them coming back time and again for more. Her favorite genre is paranormal romance, with a great deal of spice. You can visit Kathi online and drop her an email if you'd like. She loves hearing from her fans. aaronskiss@gmail.com.

Follow Kathi on her blog: http://kathisbartonauthor.blogspot.com/

www.ingramcontent.com/pod-product-compliance
Lightning Source LLC
Chambersburg PA
CBHW030224180626
46810CB00008B/2950